In the
company
of
Crazies

Other books by
NORA RALEIGH BASKIN

BASKETBALL (OR SOMETHING LIKE IT)
ALMOST HOME
WHAT EVERY GIRL (EXCEPT ME) KNOWS

Nora Raleigh Baskin

In the Company of Crazies

ILLUSTRATED BY
HENRY P. RALEIGH

HarperCollins *Publishers*

A perfect friend and a perfect first reader—
Are always honest,
Are always kind,
And always believe in you.
Jill Becker has been both for me, for a very very long time.

I also want to thank Maria Modugno, my editor, who seems to truly hear what I am trying to say.

And Nancy Gallt, my agent, who encourages me to "say it" any way I can.

Of course, Steve, Ben, and Sam—I love you with all my heart.

In the Company of Crazies
Text copyright © 2006 by Nora Raleigh Baskin
Illustrations copyright © 2006 by Henry P. Raleigh
All rights reserved. Printed in the United States of America. No part of this book may be used or reproduced in any manner whatsoever without written permission except in the case of brief quotations embodied in critical articles and reviews. For information address HarperCollins Children's Books, a division of HarperCollins Publishers, 1350 Avenue of the Americas, New York, NY 10019.
www.harpercollinschildrens.com

Library of Congress Cataloging-in-Publication Data
Baskin, Nora Raleigh.
    In the company of crazies / by Nora Raleigh Baskin ; illustrated by Henry P. Raleigh.—1st ed.
        p.   cm.
    Summary: Troubled thirteen-year-old Mia Singer enrolls in the Mountain Laurel School for Alternative Education, where she learns a lot about herself by paying close attention to others.
    ISBN-10: 0-06-059607-4 (trade bdg.) — ISBN-13: 978-0-06-059607-1 (trade bdg.)
    ISBN-10: 0-06-059608-2 (lib. bdg.) — ISBN-13: 978-0-06-059608-8 (lib. bdg.)
    [1. Juvenile delinquents—Fiction. 2. Boarding schools—Fiction. 3. Schools—Fiction.] I. Raleigh, Henry P., ill. II. Title.
PZ7.B29233Inat 2006   2005018568
[Fic]—dc22   CIP
                                                                                              AC

Typography by Karin Paprocki
1 2 3 4 5 6 7 8 9 10
❖
First Edition

For my dad

Part One

Mountain Laurel, the middle of
nowhere and nothing.

One of the teachers here, Karen,
says I am supposed to write in this
journal every day. That's about all
they have to do here and half of them
don't even do it.

What do I have to say? And if I did,
why would I want someone to read it?

I have nothing to say.

All I have to say is —
Nothing.

Going to Mountain Laurel was my choice. That's what they told me. *They.* The collective *they.* My therapist. My school counselor. The entire middle-school guidance department. My dad. And my mom, who was the one who found this place to begin with. The only one who didn't want me to go was my little sister, Cecily. But Cecily was eight and what did she know?

I *agreed* to go.

They needed to hear that.

They needed to believe that it had been my choice. But by the time everyone came to the conclusion that boarding school would be the best solution for *all* of us, it was the middle of October and most places had, at least, a year waiting list. And exactly whose fault *that* was became just another matter for a huge debate. A brawl, really. Whose fault was it that we had waited so long, hadn't read the signs, didn't seek professional help until it was nearly too late? It made for some real good fights between my mom and dad. Some real doozies. But by that time, I was used to them fighting about me. Fighting about my grades (dropping by the minute), my friends (or lack thereof), shoplifting (getting *caught* shoplifting), my skipping school (a lot).

No, by this time I was practically a war veteran. They could have paraded me through the streets on Memorial Day.

Their fighting didn't even faze me at all.

But Cecily hated it. She would hide under her bed because that's where our dog, Morgan, went as soon as he sensed someone's voice getting too loud, too angry. And that's where he stayed until it got quiet again. Dogs are funny like that. They can just feel it coming. Cecily was just following Morgan.

"Everybody knows these schools fill up way in advance." (My mother.)

"Everybody? Who is everybody? Who is everybody?" (My father.) "And what's your goddamn point anyway? I really can't see your point."

But Mountain Laurel hadn't filled up. They were accepting girls for the first time and the changeover had created a spot.

An opening.

I needed an opening. (And Cecily needed to come out from under her bed.) I needed an out. I needed an escape. So I went.

So I guess it was my decision after all.

Mountain Laurel was a farm, or at least it must have been at one time. When my dad first drove into the place, I thought we had made a mistake. There was a huge barn. There was a little beach and a pond, and behind that was a hill and pine trees all lined up like they had been planted that way. The house looked like an old farmhouse, white with reddish brown shutters on almost all the windows and a front porch piled with split fire-wood. A big white husky dog sat watching us. There were those Adirondack chairs scattered on the front lawn, lots of them in a semicircle, like people had just been sitting there a minute ago, talking.

The whole place was laid out like a mini–colonial village. Like an old-fashioned Amish community. Like something from another time. My dad and I both sat in the car for a while, just looking out, wondering if we were in the right place.

"The sign said Mountain Laurel," I said to my dad.

"It did, didn't it?" he said, nodding. But neither one of us moved.

* * *

Mountain Laurel

When I don't feel like writing,
which is all the time, Karen says I
can just draw. I can doodle something
instead.

Which is what I'm going to do.

It wasn't just the shoplifting that got me sent away, but funny it would turn out to be the Mountain Laurel School for Alternative Education. Because when my mother searched *Mountain Laurel* on the Internet and found out that it had once been categorized as a school for "emotionally disturbed adolescent boys" she was a little hesitant, to put it mildly.

Well, forget for a minute that I wasn't a boy—I *was* an adolescent, I'm often accused of being too emotional and my parents are completely disturbed. So put it all together and you have a perfect match. But did it really matter at that point anyway?

"I don't know," my mother said. "It was a *boys'* school."

"So what?" I remember telling my mother.

I remember telling her that but not thinking about it. It was almost an instinct by then. I had developed a bunch of phrases, all more or less guaranteed to end any conversation.

I don't care.

Shut up.

You're annoying me.

So what?

Eventually, my mother convinced herself that it was their old website and the school wasn't like that anymore. After all, they were accepting girls now. They had changed their name. Their brochure claimed superior education (she latched on to that one big-time) and they had an immediate opening. Besides, like I said, it wasn't just the shoplifting. I think ultimately it was that phone message I left on the attendance secretary's answering machine.

I used to be real good at deepening my voice just a bit and very seriously saying something like, "Mia Singer, grade seven, will be absent today. She has an orthodontist appointment."

Or a sore throat.

Or a family emergency.

But that day, for some reason, I said something completely different. I said, "Mia Singer won't be able to come to school today because she's dead."

The shoplifting was just the icing on the cake.

"It doesn't look like a school," my dad said.

I looked out the window. "I think that's the point."

We were far enough north to notice that the trees here had already begun to transform. The late-morning sun filtered down through the big red leaves onto the tops of the buildings and set them on fire. We were late. We were supposed to have gotten here first thing in the morning. Eight a.m. Breakfast and cleanup would be done and the first class began at 8:15, my dad had been told. But it had been more than an hour's drive and had taken a little longer to leave the house than we had planned. It took my mother a long time to say good-bye and, when it came right down to it, she couldn't. Cecily was under the bed again.

To the right of the farmhouse was a long, flat rectangle building, one story, with windows all along the side and two big black doors. The path through the grass from the house to the two black doors was worn down to dirt.

And then suddenly someone came out of the rectangle building. A little someone.

"You're here!"

My dad must have recognized the woman. He opened his car door without saying anything to me.

"Yes, we're here. Sorry we're late," he began.

I didn't like this woman right away and I changed my mind immediately about coming here. In fact, this didn't seem like a good idea at all. I thought I'd be much better off at my regular school. I'd go back. I'd stay there. I'd buckle down and get serious. After all, that was the guidance counselor's original suggestion. When did I agree to this? I certainly hadn't. Not this.

What was I thinking? I wasn't thinking.

I felt the tears burning inside my face. I felt that really sharp, deep pain that sticks you right in your throat.

I heard the word *no* shouting inside my brain, but nothing came out.

My dad walked around and opened my door. He never opens the door for me, but when he did I got out of the car, because I didn't know what else to do.

"This is Mia," he said to the woman.

I couldn't look up. I knew I would cry.

"Hello, Mia. It's nice to meet you," she said. "I am Gretchen."

The woman had a foreign accent, German or Russian or French or something, and it made me feel even farther from home. She was shorter than me. I decided I was never going to like anything about her.

"At Mountain Laurel, when someone speaks to you, it's polite to respond," she said.

No, I would always hate everything about her.

I turned to my dad, but he wasn't looking at me. There are those certain times when doing what you're told seems like your only choice, and this seemed like one of those times.

"Hello," I mumbled.

I started listening to what she was saying about schedules, phone calls, and getting picked up, but I noticed faces at the window behind her. Boys, about five or six of them, all pushed up to the glass, watching. One face was long, with pimples and light-colored hair on top. Next to him was a dark-haired boy with a round face. And there was a big boy with nearly a man's face, but there was something odd about his expression, alert but confused. Next to him was a skinny face, his eyes darting around, his lips talking. There was a boy with a baby face and blond, blond hair.

There were more faces that moved to and from the window so quickly, I couldn't see them all.

"Those are the boys. The other students here," Gretchen said when she noticed me watching. "You'll meet them soon enough. Come. Let's get your things."

My dad took my suitcase out of the trunk and started to carry it toward the house, but Gretchen stopped him.

"She can do that, Mr. Singer. It's time for you to say good-bye," she said. "It's almost time for period two. We are already behind schedule. I will call you tonight as I told you I would."

This time my father looked at me. *He can't do this,* I thought. *He's not going to just leave. Just because this midget Nazi told him to.*

"It will be fine, Mia. I'll talk to you soon," my dad said. "I love you."

He stepped toward me like he wanted to hug, but I turned away. I didn't say anything. He couldn't have it both ways. He couldn't. I could make sure he felt bad the whole way home, but as he drove away I knew I was going to feel worse than he would.

A lot worse.

Mountain Laurel.
Karen says if you don't want anyone, mainly her, to read what you've written in your journal, you

just fold that page over. Which is really stupid, because as soon as you fold over the page, you're going to look like you're hiding something. So then you probably are.

The very first time I ever shoplifted, it really *was* because I wanted something. Believe it or not, it was a bottle of perfume. It was more than a year ago. I was only twelve. I didn't even *wear* perfume. I still don't wear perfume. It makes me sneeze and besides, it's not like me at all. I'm more like the Nike-wearing, ponytail-and-hooded-sweatshirt type.

I was at the mall with my best friend, Marcella. It was our first trip to the mall by ourselves. Well, by ourselves with two cell phones and explicit directions. My mother told me to call home every hour on the hour. At the top of every half hour, we had to call Marcella's mother.

I had fifty dollars in my wallet. I knew Marcella had more.

At first we just walked around, poking into stores and walking around some more. I had been to the mall millions of times with my mom, but somehow it seemed like there was more stuff there that day. There was anything I wanted. Anything within fifty dollars, that is, minus tax. Minus lunch.

"I'm hungry; are you?" Marcella said after about an hour of window-shopping and our first two phone calls.

"Not really." But just thinking about eating made me hungry when only a second ago I wasn't. "But I'll go with you," I said. My stomach growled.

By the time we found the food court, I was starving. I think if she had gotten Chinese food or something, I probably would have shared with her. But Marcella got a slice of pizza and a soda. I got a drink of water and, as it was, that cost me twenty-five cents for the Styrofoam cup.

"It's okay. I told you I wasn't hungry," I insisted for the second time. I was already down to $49.75.

I saw the bottle of perfume at one of those kiosk cart things in the middle of the mall. There was just one girl sitting there on a stool, looking really bored. She had all sorts of stuff on her cart, mostly hair accessories—headbands and barrettes. There were long hair extensions in all colors, natural and unnatural, hanging from the top shelf. And on the far end, away from the girl on her stool, were bottles of perfume.

Marcella was trying on a crocheted hat and looking at herself in the little mirror that was propped up between the hair combs and the glitter powder. I wasn't about to waste my money on something junky, so I wandered around the four sides of the cart while Marcella tried to make up her mind.

The silver and blue cylinder-shaped bottle caught my eye. I had seen the advertisements for that perfume on TV lots of times. In the TV commercial this young woman, kind of an older teenage girl, is walking down the street in Paris with her hair swinging from side to side.

I don't even think I *wanted* the perfume until I saw it sitting there. Then all I could think of was the girl in the commercial, the music, and everyone looking at her thinking she was so beautiful and confident.

The price for all the perfumes in that section was masking-taped to the shelf: $24.99.

It's not like I'm so dumb. I didn't think I'd be transported to the streets of France and my hair would suddenly go from dark and wavy to blond and straight and swing from side to side behind me. There was just something that made me want that perfume.

Twenty-four ninety-nine was more than I was willing to spend, especially for something I didn't need. I knew other girls who stole things. I was in the pharmacy once, the one right in town, and I watched Chrissy Babcock drop a 3 Musketeers bar into her coat pocket.

When she got outside, all her friends circled around her, laughing and cheering.

It seemed so easy. And nobody got hurt.

Marcella must still have been looking at herself in the mirror. I could tell by her voice coming from the other side of the cart that she really liked the hat. The girl on the stool seemed to agree, although she hadn't budged off her perch. I took the silver bottle and held it in my hands.

I just wanted it. I wanted something. Something I couldn't have. So I let it slip right out of my hand and gently into my pocket, where it quietly remained for the rest of my time in the mall, all the way home in the car with Marcella's mom, and all the way up to my room. I felt excited. And scared. And sick. All at the same time.

I never opened the perfume bottle, never broke the plastic seal. I didn't dare put it out on my shelf, where it might have looked pretty at least, because someone might have seen it.

I didn't want to use it because I don't like perfume but also because then I'd use it up. I hid it in a plastic bag, in a shoe box in the back of my closet.

I still have it.

Honest.

* * *

"Everyone, I'd like you to meet Mia," Gretchen said, like it was a big announcement, and even though I figured she would do something like that, I sunk down in my seat. We were all sitting at this really long table, in the dining room.

I had spent most of the day with Karen, who was one of the teachers at Mountain Laurel. I mean, I guess she was a teacher. She was an adult anyway. First, Karen showed me around the farmhouse, Gretchen's house. She pointed out the bathroom and Gretchen's office; both were locked. She explained that all the teachers had a key for the bathroom. She took me outside and into the long classroom building where I had first seen all the faces and then across the way to the nursery school. That's where my room was, on a renovated floor above the nursery school. When (if?) other girls joined the school, we would share this room. It was big enough. There were three empty beds.

Karen had the room across the hall from mine. There was a bathroom (unlocked) and shower between us. The stairs leading up actually passed right through the nursery school. I could see the little kids busy playing and coloring and building with blocks. I almost walked right by. I didn't notice it right away, but something out of the corner of my eye told me this scene was not quite right.

On our way back out, I made it a point to look more closely. These kids all had problems, real problems — the kind of problems you can see and hear if you listen. Some clearly had Down's syndrome, and I wondered how I could have missed that on my way in. A couple of the kids were wearing helmets. One boy was in a wheelchair.

By now it was five o'clock, time to come into Gretchen's house for dinner.

It wasn't until I was inside, finally left alone to think a minute, that I realized this wasn't a school that looked like someone's house; rather, it was someone's house that looked very little like a school, which was infinitely worse. And it only remotely looked like a school because there was more of everything. The table had a lot more chairs around it. The kitchen had more stacks of plates and more cups. The stove had more burners. The mudroom had a long row of hooks, coats and jackets. On the floor were scattered lots and lots of ratty shoes.

Which was another awful thing.

You had to take off your shoes when you came into the house. Nobody wore shoes in Gretchen's house except Gretchen. She had a pair of shoes that looked like little worn-out Chinese slippers.

I hate not having my shoes on.

I don't know what it is or when it started. I'm sure I

went barefoot when I was a baby, just like every other baby. But somewhere along the line I came to hate bare feet. Even in the summer, I wear shoes. I don't even like sandals. I like socks. With shoes on top of them.

But not in Gretchen's house.

Mountain Laurel.
Everybody here is crazy.
Maybe I'll fit right in.

So the reason everyone got upset about my phone call to the attendance secretary wasn't just because I, obviously, wasn't dead and therefore should have been in school. The reason everyone got really upset with me was because on that day one year before, there *was* someone who had died in my school.

Debbie Sanders.

I didn't know Debbie very well. Hardly at all. She

was in the grade above me. We lived on the same street so she rode my bus. Or I rode *her* bus. And we were both on the middle-school volleyball team. Debbie died in a "freak" car accident. That's what they call it when somebody dies when nobody should have. As if there could be a kind of car accident where somebody *should* die. But you know when there's an accident and everybody is so relieved because they say, if the car had been just one fraction of an inch to the left or the right, or if it had happened a second earlier or a second later or whatever, they would have hit that tree and died?

Well, Debbie's accident *was* that one fraction of an inch and that single second. And she died.

A freak accident.

Nobody knew it until the next morning, though. She was one of about fifteen of us who were supposed to show up at the VFW that night for the fund-raising ziti dinner. She was actually one of two kids who didn't come.

Joanne Murphy and her mom weren't there either.

Everyone on the girls' volleyball team had sold tickets to the dinner, ten dollars a plate. Then all the parents donated the food and the players cooked and served it that night. Each of us got a big round table to wait on, and even though there was only one choice—ziti—it was still kind of fun. Like playing restaurant. There were more girls than tables, so when Debbie Sanders and Joanne Murphy didn't show up, it actually worked out better. Every girl got to wait on her own table.

There was a ton of work to do and we had to do it really fast. The dinner started at 6:30. The moms were cooking pasta like crazy, and most of us were setting up the tables. We had to drag the heavy chairs from where they were stacked up against the wall. Twelve place settings at every table. Plastic utensils wrapped in a paper napkin. A tall plastic cup and one glass Parmesan cheese dispenser. (The VFW let us use theirs.) Then, when the people started showing up, it got even more hectic. Every girl was running around, filling up glasses of lemonade and plates of ziti. It was advertised as "all you can eat," which I had never really understood until that night. Some people really like to take advantage of that.

Nobody had time to call Debbie or Joanne.

It turned out that Joanne Murphy was doing her homework and she just forgot all about it.

"It was last night?" she said the next day in school. "I can't believe it. I had my tennis lesson. Then my math tutor. I just completely forgot!"

"Yeah, right," Marcella said. "The whole team is really furious with you."

Which was true for a few minutes that morning, until we found out what happened to Debbie Sanders. Then nobody cared that Joanne Murphy had crapped out on the all-you-can-eat ziti dinner.

"Stand up, Mia," Gretchen said. She raised her hands in the air and gestured up and down like she thought she could move things with just her will.

"Come now. Stand up." It was an order apparently. I think everything Gretchen said was an order. And I noticed already that everyone obeyed. Even the grown-ups.

I stood up.

It was pretty dark in the dining room. There were a few lights in the living room, but only one table lamp was on, and only one dim light hung from the ceiling above the dining table. It was definitely one of those houses where they are always worrying about money and trying to save energy because it was cold, like the heat was down. Way down. My feet were freezing.

Still, I could see all the faces looking right at me. The same faces I saw through the window in the rectangle building. They called that the School House. The main building, what I first thought was a farmhouse, Gretchen's house, where the boys' rooms were upstairs, where we were now sitting down to eat dinner, was simply called the House. As if there were no other house in the world.

The House.

"I want everyone to meet Mia," Gretchen said.

"Hi, Mia." One of the boys said it first. I recognized his face. The round face with the dark hair. Now I could see he had freckles and he looked about twelve or thirteen. Maybe fourteen. He smiled too big and totally insincerely. He was sitting across from me, a few boys down.

I felt my face heating up. To ease the focus of everyone on me, I made a mental tally of who was in the room. There were six, seven, eight, nine boys in total. Karen, the teacher who had taken me on my grand tour, sat at one end. Another teacher, a man, flanked the boys at the other end of the table. Gretchen sat at the head, near the kitchen, and the woman who had cooked dinner beside her. Thirteen in total.

No, fourteen. Counting me.

I really just wanted my shoes back and on my feet.

"Hi," another boy said. He looked younger. Frailer than the other boys. He was blond and thin and when he smiled it seemed real. He also seemed nervous, very nervous. So I smiled back.

"Hi," I said.

"That was Tommy," Gretchen said. "And Drew." She nodded to the nervous boy.

"I'm Billy."

Billy was kind of chubby and he looked very young. Billy smiled and waved to me, but as soon as he could get his hand back into his mouth he did. He started biting his nails.

Gretchen went down the table like that. Everyone was introduced and then said hello. The man teacher was Mr. Simone. He was the only one who was called by his last name. And his name wasn't *Simone* like *Simon says*. It was Simone with three syllables, like *ba-lon-ey*. *Si-mon-e*.

There was one really huge boy, and the huge boy was really strange. His shirt was buttoned all the way to the top and he hadn't talked until Gretchen made him. When he did, he sounded very formal and stiff. He had a big square head, too, that matched his voice. He looked like Frankenstein. His name was John, but that's the way I was going to remember him — Frankenstein. It's not that I was mean or that I gave a shit. It was more like reading road signs: SLIPPERY WHEN WET, BUMP, HIDDEN DRIVE. They're necessary to stay alive, assuming that is your objective.

Gretchen directed the whole thing. Everybody

answered. Everybody said hello, but you could tell who was doing it sarcastically, because the other boys smirked or laughed, and who meant it. So far, I thought only Drew had meant it. Maybe that boy Billy, who was still biting his nails. Another boy at the far end only nodded when Gretchen introduced him. His name was Angel. Gretchen pronounced it differently, but everyone else just called him Angel, as in angel.

"Is Mia going to be my roommate?" one of the boys, Tommy, I think, asked, which got a big laugh and a lot of rude noises.

"There's an extra bed in my room," Carl said. He was the boy with the pimples. That was how I was going to remember him. It was obvious Tommy and Carl were friends. And leaders.

"If she were in your bed, you wouldn't know what to do," Tommy said.

"We all know *you* would," Carl shot back. "We hear you practicing every night."

Gretchen stood up.

"Enough," she said sharply.

They were really not much different from the boys at my old school on any given bad day, on any given lunchroom afternoon, during any football game, in any locker room, bathroom, hallway when they think no grown-ups are listening.

The only difference was these boys didn't seem to care that grown-ups were listening. Grown-ups were sitting right at the table. *I* was sitting right at the table.

"You're all very funny," Gretchen said. "One more comment like that and you'll be sleeping outside. All week."

You got the feeling she was the type to follow through with her threats.

And it all got very quiet.

School had always come pretty easy to me. I was kind of a teacher favorite almost all the way to seventh grade, before things kind of fell apart. I don't think I ever *didn't* get 100 percent on a spelling test, if not on the pretest, then certainly on the Friday spelling test. In sixth grade I got moved up for math and put into the highest reading group. At my parent/teacher conference they said it was highly unusual for a student to excel in both math *and* language arts.

But that was me.

And my parents loved it. I mean, they pretended it wasn't such a big deal. But my mom couldn't wait to ask me how I did if she knew I'd had a test that day. It got to the point I could tell when she was trying *not* to ask, trying not to put too much pressure on me to do well. I could tell because she'd ask me about something stupid when I got home from school, while I was sitting having my snack. She'd talk about something totally opposite from what she really wanted to know.

I got new pillows for the guest-room bed, she'd say. *Did you notice them?*

Or:

Daddy is really due for an oil change in his car. Maybe tomorrow he can take mine so I can run it over to the garage for him.

I could literally feel her waiting.

She'd wait all afternoon.

And eventually I'd tell her because I used to love her reaction. I loved her big smile and the way she'd look at me. It made me feel good.

But then one day, it didn't.

It happened slowly. In sixth grade, we started

switching classes and teachers, and things were a little different. I was taking seventh-grade pre-algebra. It was hard and the teacher didn't really like me.

I got my first detention ever from that teacher. I had to stay in for recess and she sent a note home to my parents informing them that I had received a detention. I thought I was going to throw up when that letter came in the mail.

But the real change was at home. I don't remember when it first became so clear to me that my mother cared more than I did. But it was sometime during that sixth-grade year.

"Don't you have a math test tomorrow?" my mother asked me. She was doing the dishes or folding laundry or something like that.

"Yeah," I said. I was watching a rerun of *Friends*.

"Do you want me to study with you?" She kept working on what she happened to be doing, folding or rinsing or wiping the counter. Trying so hard to appear only casually interested.

"No."

"Daddy will be home soon. He's better at math than me anyway," she said. It was driving her crazy.

This time I didn't say anything. I didn't respond at all. I just stared at the TV.

"Mia, did you hear me?"

I had heard her, of course. My inside was fighting with my outside because I felt like I should be studying too. My outside was watching TV. My legs were comfortable. My neck was comfortable. I didn't want to move, get up, and drag my fifty-pound backpack onto the couch and dig for my math book.

My inside was worrying about the test the next day. Exponents and negative numbers, balancing equations. *I should read the chapter again*, I thought. *I should get up.* Maybe my mother could test me from my homework.

But it didn't happen like that.

My mother walked into the den, right in front of me, and flipped off the TV.

"Enough," she said. "It's time to study."

I was so surprised for a second I just sat there. To be honest, I didn't think I was going to turn the TV back on, lay on the couch for the whole night, and never study one page. At first, I didn't even consider that.

But there was something in her face.

Or her body, the way she was standing there, blocking the cable box so I couldn't use the remote. Her hands were wet because (now I remember) she was doing the dishes. She must have just put the dishwashing detergent in the little thingy, flipped the handle, and started the machine.

I could hear the steady hum of the dishwasher.

She had a dish towel in her hand. She was standing and I was sitting. She was the grown-up and I was the kid, but I suddenly realized I was more powerful than she was. And it terrified me.

"I don't need to," I said. "I know it all." I leaned over with the clicker to get around her body and pointed it at the box. The sound of the TV filled the space between us.

I'm not saying that's all it was. I'm not saying I slipped right off the deep end that very afternoon, but it was the beginning and it was the end.

I know there are plenty of kids whose parents check their homework every night and make them redo it. I know a girl in my class whose father and mother come into the school and demand to see the list of books that will be assigned for the year. And then they refuse to let their daughter waste her time on books below her reading level.

They slash off *Island of the Blue Dolphins*.

They draw lines through *My Brother Sam Is Dead* and *Sarah, Plain and Tall* and *Bud, Not Buddy*.

And they write their own list that looks like a high-school syllabus: *Johnny Tremain, A Raisin in the*

Sun, and *Julius Caesar.*

I've heard of parents who have their kids tutored all summer and all school year, every week, unwilling to leave anything to chance. Intent on making sure their kids have every advantage. Even (no, especially) the kids in the top reading and math classes. It's not about getting help, it's about staying ahead.

Then, at some point while I was pretending not to care, I really didn't. I'm not saying it only had to do with my math teacher, my grades, or that detention, or my mother, or Debbie Sanders, who was probably doing homework right up to the minute before she left for the ziti dinner.

I'm not saying anything.

It was so cold at Mountain Laurel. Cold every-where, but colder inside than out. And much colder at night. I had the kind of bed they give you at sleep-away camp, with metal springs and a flimsy, striped mattress that is so hideous you have to cover it right away with a top sheet, hoping you'll forget what it looks like when you're lying on it at night.

I was freezing. I pulled my blanket up to my chin and made sure no pockets of air could slip in from anywhere. I didn't remember ever being this lonely before. Or this cold.

My mattress was so lumpy and thin. All I could do was lie there and count the nights until the weekend. I knew that most of the boarders at Mountain Laurel went home on Friday and came back Sunday afternoon. But when I went home I was going to tell my mom, "Never. No way. Not in a million years am I going to go back there."

My mom always came through, no matter how mad she was at me. No matter how mad I was at her.

I'm sure she missed me. I bet she was crying right now, thinking about me. It made me feel a little better to think that she was feeling as bad as I was. I was sure she was.

Karen was in the room right across the hall. She was nice enough. That night, she made sure I had everything I needed: sheets, blankets, towels, soap. Mountain Laurel provided all that. She was telling me about the schedule and then about how she came to work here and why she loved it. She was trying to make me comfortable, I suppose.

"I used to teach in the real world." She laughed. "I was a high school English teacher. AP exams, SATIIs, tutoring. The whole works. It's different here. You'll see. It's safe here. It's peaceful."

I thought that was an odd adjective for this place, but I didn't say so.

"I'm right across the hall if you need me." Karen pointed.

"Thanks," I said. I did want to ask her some things. What about the bathroom? What time did we have to get up? Was Gretchen always so mean? How could Karen like it here? Then, all of a sudden, Karen looked really tired. I recognized the look in her face, so I told her it had been a long day and I probably should go to bed. She said that was a good idea and she went into her room and I went into the other room. The nursery school was dark. As we came up, I had noticed the tiny chairs all standing upside down on top of the tiny tables, just like any regular nursery school. Almost.

Karen was still awake, I think. I could see a little light slipping under my door. Other than that, it was black. There were no lights on outside. I sat up and looked out the window.

From my window I could see the main house, Gretchen's house, *the* House. All the lights were out except for a little porch light and one tiny light in one of the downstairs windows. I thought it was that same table lamp in the living room, beside the armchair. They told me that was Gretchen's chair. No one else could sit there.

I saw the dog, curled up on the porch. It just figured she'd make her dog sleep outside. The ground outside looked hardened, ready for winter. The grass, with the circle of wooden chairs, sat still. The School House was dark, all the windows black.

The nursery school was the tallest building, so from this window I could almost see past the School House and to the top of the pond. I could just see the far end of where the beach would be and the hill of pine trees beyond that. Everything was shadowy gray and quiet. Only the stars and a thin moon breaking through a cloudy night sky lit the ground. It looked unreal, so silent and still.

And so cold.

I got undressed under the covers, down to my underwear and T-shirt. I kept my socks on. I threw my sweatpants and sweatshirt into the corner of the room, on the floor, where they lay in the dark. Just like me.

I was just about to lie back down on my bed when I saw a tiny light go on in the House on the top floor, toward the back, where I knew the boys' rooms were. The dorms, Karen had called them. I strained my eyes. Someone was in that room, walking around. I could see movement. I pressed my nose to the cold glass but my breath fogged up the window. There was definitely someone looking out that window.

I pulled my face back and rubbed a little opening clean. Yes, someone was there looking right back at me. I couldn't tell who it was, but it was definitely not a grown-up. I watched and they watched and then slowly the figure put up a hand to the window and I did the same. I could feel the cold against my fingertips.

It made me shiver all down my back, and I dropped down onto my bed and lay perfectly still. I didn't look again. I must have fallen asleep because the next thing I knew it was morning.

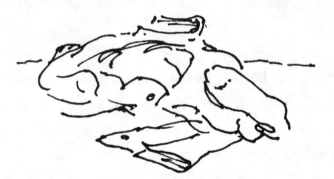

I had been shoplifting for a long time before I got caught. I mean, *really* caught. There had been plenty of near misses. Or some times when I just put something back because I felt so bad.

"Oh, that color would look great on you."

"Huh?"

"I saw you looking at the shirt," the girl said. "I think you'd look really good in it." She didn't look much older than me. And she wasn't your usual snobby, what-is-someone-like-you-doing-in-this-store kind of salesgirl. She was nice. I could just tell.

She didn't know—I mean, I didn't *think* she knew—that I had a halter top and a little plastic jar of beads in my pocket. The beads were pretty and small and they were sitting in a basket near the back of the store, on the floor. Easy to bend down and stand up again with the beads hidden in my hand. The halter top was just small and sitting on a shelf, just the perfect height of my hand and my pocket.

I would never wear it. It wasn't even my size.

"I think it's a good color for you," the girl said again.

I had to look at the rack of shirts that I had just been pretending to look through. I never just ran out of a store after I slipped something in my pocket. I wandered around a little while, looking at different things, trying to look as if I was really looking for something. It also gave me time to put something back if I thought someone was watching me. I could always say I was just holding it.

I was *going* to pay for it.

Of course.

But this girl wasn't watching me. She was just talking. Trying to make a sale maybe. Or maybe she was a little bored. A little lonely.

"Oh, thanks," I said. I looked at the shirt. It was a soft, cottony, light blue, long-sleeved T-shirt. The kind of shirt that you don't really want but you buy it and it becomes your favorite. You wear it all the time and the older it gets, the better it looks. I felt kind of sick.

"Do you want to try it on? They're on sale," the girl said, smiling.

"Yeah, sure."

The girl sprung off her chair and went to unlock one of the dressing rooms. When she got back she must have seen the bottle of beads and the halter top on the counter, but I don't think she thought anything about that.

I felt terrible all day.

When I got caught for real, at Kohl's department store, I was in possession of a pair of gray angora gloves and a green fake leather belt with silver studs.

I realized at breakfast that whoever had been at the window knew who I was but I didn't know who he was. We were back at the long table again. I tried to look at some of the faces to see if I could find a sign. It was quieter in the morning. Some of the boys had wet hair. There was a strong smell of soap and sporty-scented deodorant. Most everyone looked sleepy. It was 7:00. If someone here had waved to me last night, he wasn't letting me know. Maybe he had told everyone. Maybe they were all laughing at me. I knew what boys said. I knew the kind of things they made up. And these boys were worse than most.

Breakfast was the same scenario as the night before. Same Gretchen at the head of the table. Only this time, Karen was at the other end. The cook woman was in the kitchen. I guess the other teacher, Mr. Simone, didn't live here. He wasn't at the table.

Same blue and green hard plastic dishes, same boys. I had the same feeling that none of this was real. Only maybe a little stronger than I felt last night. And we were having oatmeal and toast and sliced bananas. And if possible, it was even colder than last night. My toes were numb.

Gretchen informed me that we were allowed to get up from the table and go into the kitchen for seconds. Firsts, however, had to be sent down the line, passed from person to person. And no one was allowed to eat until everyone had their food.

I actually like oatmeal and I wanted seconds. And it did feel like that scene from *Oliver Twist*.

Please, sir. I want some more.

But not really. The woman in the kitchen looked nice.

"So you like my oatmeal," she said.

I nodded and I tried to smile, but it was hard.

She ladled out the hot cereal. Just the steam from my bowl hitting my face felt warm and good. It was lighter in the kitchen too. There were windows and sunlight.

"I'm Maggie," she told me.

"I'm Mia."

"Hello, Mia," she said. "It's nice to have a girl around here for a change."

I didn't know what to say but I wanted to stay in the kitchen a little longer. I needed to start a little conversation. I thought I would say something, like maybe about the weather or about how my mother made oatmeal, which she didn't. But suddenly the Frankenstein boy with the stiff voice walked in and stood right behind me. He had his bowl in his hand. He was taller than I realized last night when he was sitting at the dinner table. And he was big. Not just a big head, but a big chest and big legs. He wore his shirt tightly tucked in and his belt pulled a notch too far. His boots were big.

"Uh, excuse me," he said to me.

"Oh, sorry." I quickly stepped aside. John held out his bowl to Maggie.

"I can have my seconds now, Maggie," he said. I imagine that was how Frankenstein would talk.

"Well, here you go then, John," Maggie said. She filled his bowl.

"Thank you, Maggie. But, Maggie, I have to say . . . ," John started.

Maggie paused to listen, and so did I. I just stood there.

"I noticed you forgot to put the salt in the oatmeal this morning. You never do that, Maggie. Why did you? Did you forget? Didn't you read the lid of the box? It says right there on the box. One fourth teaspoon of salt. It's the same every time. There is no reason to change that." He spoke very fast.

"You didn't like it, John?" Maggie asked him.

"No, Maggie. I did not."

"Then why do you want more?"

"I mean, I can eat it but—"

Maggie interrupted him. "Why don't you just enjoy your breakfast, John."

"It's in the recipe. On the lid of the box . . ." John's voice grew stronger.

"I put the salt in the oatmeal," Maggie said firmly. "Now go in and sit down."

As soon as John had left the kitchen, Maggie looked over to me and winked.

"Now, how the heck can he taste that?" she whispered to me. "One fourth of a teaspoon? How does he know?" She was smiling and shaking her head. She made it a little easier—I smiled back.

I thought Maggie looked older, not quite like a grandmother but older than a mom. But normal, definitely normal. I wondered why she was here. How do you get a job cooking three meals a day in a school for emotionally disturbed adolescent boys? John was lumbering back into the dining room.

"Maggie didn't put the salt in the oatmeal," he was saying to no one in particular. "The recipe calls for salt. One fourth teaspoon. Is that too hard? I know she didn't put it in."

I watched as Carl slid his chair out just the tiniest bit so John, who was concentrating on the saltless oatmeal in his bowl, nearly tripped. He took two flying steps, balanced himself, but dropped his oatmeal.

Make that emotionally disturbed adolescent boys and a couple of sociopaths.

* * *

Mountain Laurel.

It's awful here. Awful and horrible and cold.

Deeply, deeply cold.

We found out before the second bell rang that Debbie Sanders had died. It was the most awful day. It went on forever, and then the next morning I woke up thinking it had all been a dream. I know that sounds really cliché, but it was true.

And then you clear your head and you remember.

Somehow I couldn't get it out of my mind that she had been dead already while we were forking out saucy ziti and pouring seconds of lemonade. It seemed so wrong that we didn't know. That we didn't stop. That everyone just ate and talked and even got mad that she wasn't there. Then we went home and did our homework, worried about some test or another, some boy or another, brushed our teeth and went to bed.

And Debbie was already dead.

Most of the seventh graders called their parents, and a lot of them went home that day. Whoever was left didn't go to classes. When the bell rang and the rest of us in sixth grade came out into the halls, we could see girls crying, leaning on their lockers. Even boys were crying. And everyone was talking.

"I heard the driver just walked away without a scratch."

"It must have been a deer."

"They were arguing in the car."

". . . talking on the cell phone."

". . . changing the radio station."

I knew immediately that we would never find out the truth. That even if the details got straightened out and the rumors fell away, it would never, never ever, make sense. There was a feeling that nothing would ever be all right again.

At the end of that day we had an assembly. I had never heard it so quiet in the auditorium. By then it was pretty empty, too. The principal, vice principal, and the two school counselors (the following year I would be seeing a lot more of all four of them) were standing on the stage. Mr. Leighy, the principal, walked up to the microphone and began.

"I'm sure by now most of you have heard the tragic news. Debbie Sanders, a seventh grader in our school, was killed last night in a car accident."

When he paused you could hear the crying again.

"Mrs. Baker will be in her office for the remainder of today and for as long as she needs, to see students who wish to talk. No appointment will be necessary. Within reason, students who need this service are excused from classes. We are also sending a letter home to your parents. Make sure you give . . ."

He went on and on. Then the vice principal spoke and finally Mrs. Baker. The feeling in the room was so overwhelming. Even though the auditorium had a huge open ceiling and rows and rows of seats, I felt like I couldn't breathe.

I kept thinking about Debbie. She had died for no reason. Not even for the horrible reasons that don't make any sense either but seem nearly an explanation, like drunk driving , an icy patch, no air bags, or speeding, or not wearing a seat belt.

No, there was none of that. It was a "freak" accident. A true freak accident.

As if no matter what you did, right or wrong . . .

It didn't matter.

"It was me."

I turned around and no one was there.

We were in class, in the School House building. Half the boys I had "met" last night weren't even here. I noticed that boy Angel wasn't there.

Class.

That was what they called this? So far the only thing we were supposed to do was write in our journals. In fact, keeping a journal was the only thing everyone had to do. Karen said even she kept one. And she did seem to be writing in it. So I could do that. I could write bull-shit as good as anyone. Certainly as good as anyone here. And when I couldn't think of what to say, I could draw.

I had nothing much to say, so I drew a lot.

But it seemed that it was more like sit-around-and-talk time.

Everyone pretty much sat where they wanted. On the floor or at the table or in one of the big stuffed chairs. When we first walked in, there was a lot of fighting over one particular chair. I don't know why. One boy ran right to it, but Carl and Tommy both punched him in the arm and he got up. He seemed to be expecting it. I was waiting to see which one of them would take the seat, but neither Carl nor Tommy sat there. Karen walked in right behind us and some other boy altogether took the seat.

No one tattled, I noticed. That seemed to be an unspoken rule.

I had chosen a chair. A regular old chair pushed up to a regular rectangular table. I had even brought a notebook, but I was the only one. As soon as I noticed that, I slipped the notebook back into my bag. I kept the pen in my hand, though, so I could twiddle it in my fingers or doodle in my journal some more.

"It was me," the voice said again, and this time Drew crawled out from under a table behind me. I looked around to see if anyone else noticed or thought it was strange to be sitting under a table, but apparently no one else did.

Karen was busy trying to get Tommy to stop tormenting John. She had stood up and walked over to get in between them.

"In the window," Drew said. "Last night. I couldn't sleep. I never sleep."

"Never?"

I checked again to see if Karen was still busy, but it wouldn't have mattered. As soon as she got up to attend to Tommy, everyone else just kind of fell apart. The noise level rose instantaneously, as if her body were a volume control. Everyone started moving and talking. I think one boy just got up and left the room, out the back door. I turned completely around in my chair. Drew took a chair at the table that, a minute ago, he had been hiding under.

"Well, I suppose I sleep, because you can't live if you don't sleep, right?"

"Right," I said.

Drew must have been a year or two younger than me. But he was smaller than that. He had very blond hair, almost white, and eyelashes so light they were like snowflakes over his eyes. I had never met anyone less threatening before. It was like he was even borrowing the very space he occupied with the promise to give it back.

I was still trying to fit the names and the faces together and fill in the names I hadn't yet learned. Carl was the one with the pimples. It looked like he picked at them a lot. He even had a couple of Band-Aids, trimmed down to custom size but still covering half his forehead. Tommy had freckles and a nasty grin. Frankenstein John was big and just plain weird as could be. One of the boys kept pulling his eyebrows, so much that his left eye was practically bald. I forgot his name. Another one of the boys was chubby and wore army camouflage pants. Right, that was Billy, who bit his nails.

"Okay, everyone, calm down. Back to your seats," Karen said. She was standing by the bookshelf again. John was next to her. Tommy was slouching in his chair, smiling. The boy who had run out (I didn't know his name either) had not come back, but no one seemed to notice. Or care.

"If you have a book, take it out now," Karen said to everyone.

I didn't have a book. I looked around. Drew reached into his backpack and took out a big paperback. He started reading, but other than him, no one else had a book either.

I raised my hand, which got a big reaction.

"We're not in kindergarten," Billy said, laughing like it was the funniest thing he had ever seen.

I yanked my arm back down. I knew not to raise my hand again.

"Leave her alone, asswipe," Carl said, and when Karen wasn't looking he leaned over and punched Billy in the arm. Hard. Billy started to cry.

Carl looked at me, as if to make sure I had noticed what he must have thought was chivalry. I looked away.

I saw that most everyone just reached out and grabbed the nearest thing to read. I think Carl was reading *Better Homes and Gardens Houseplants*. John got up and headed very deliberately to one bookcase and then seemed very upset when he couldn't find what he was looking for. At which point Tommy started laughing really hard.

"Give it to me." John turned around to face Tommy. His anger had skipped some kind of preliminary stage and gone straight to fury.

"Give you what?" Tommy started.

John took his giant steps toward Tommy.

"Give it to him," Karen warned.

"Over there," Tommy said quickly, pointing. "Down there. Under. Under."

I tried to figure out if he was scared of Karen or John. I couldn't tell.

John lumbered back across the room with the small, thick paperback he had fished out from under the bookcase. When he walked by me I saw he was holding *The Guinness Book of World Records*.

Ten months after Debbie Sanders died but still a month and a half before my mother found me a prestigious spot at Mountain Laurel, I was starting seventh grade in my old school. We were supposed to read *Animal Farm*, which, by the way, I never got around to doing. I was in the highest reading group, riding on my reputation from fifth and sixth grade, I assume, because it certainly had nothing to do with my efforts so far that year. I suppose knowing that my mother was hot on the find-Mia-a boarding-school trail didn't help with my motivation.

Maybe *Animal Farm* is a good book, but I was sure if we read it in school, I would hate it.

Everyone in my group got a wrinkled-up paperback copy and an assignment: Read chapters one and two. Never read ahead. One person was supposed to write about Theme, someone else about Connections, someone else about Vocabulary. One person, believe it or not, had to draw a Picture.

At least I didn't have to draw a picture. I like drawing and I'm kind of good at it, but I'm not an A+ kind of drawer. Usually I get my mother to draw for me. She's really good at it, but she always starts out saying, "I'm not doing your homework for you, Mia."

Then I explain to her, "But it's English, not art class. Why should I get a bad grade just because I can't draw?"

Then, of course, she does it for me.

And she's not such an incredible artist that anyone ever knows. Besides, everyone has their parents make their projects for them. For fifth-grade colonial day, Lucas Spencer's homemade wig could have fooled George Washington. Johnny DiScala had real working bellows in his blacksmith shop.

For *Animal Farm*, I was supposed to do the chapter summary (chapter summaries, in my opinion, ruin any and every book). I looked down at the paperback in my hands. The top cover and about the first twenty pages or so were stuck in a sort of warped curl. I imagined all the kids before me opening the book and reading. I imagined someone before me having to write a chapter summary. And a chapter summary. And a chapter summary.

I opened the front cover of my paperback to see who had read this very same copy of *Animal Farm* before me.

The last name, in neat pencil print, was Debbie Sanders.

If I were back home I'd be in — I looked at my watch — I'd be in social studies right now. I'd be sitting at a desk in a dark room, because my seventh-grade social studies teacher, Mr. James, put everything up on the overhead projector. He had hundreds of plastic sheets filled with handwritten notes. He'd flip from one to the other and then lecture from them. You could tell he used the same ones over and over, year after year. He didn't even have to waste his energy writing on the board or thinking up new thoughts. He didn't even have to waste any chalk.

But instead I'm working in a vegetable garden.

At 10:15 in the morning.

"I forgot to tell you Gretchen's soap trick," Karen said. She was kneeling a couple of rows away. In the sun I could see she was older than I thought before. She had lots of gray hair mixed in with her long black curls, and she had wrinkles around her eyes when she smiled. In a way she looked old, but in another she looked almost my age.

"What's the soap trick?"

Karen stopped weeding. "Well, you scratch a bar of soap with your fingernails and it forces the soap underneath. It's not real comfortable but it keeps the dirt out when you're gardening," she said.

"That's okay," I said. I meant that. I wasn't sure I wanted soap forced under my fingernails.

"Next time," Karen said, and she went back to her row.

"Next time?" I asked.

Karen stood up. She rubbed her back and then stretched her arms up in the air. I could see how she had become almost part of this whole place, this garden, this school. How long had that taken? Everything that seemed so foreign to me Karen seemed so comfortable with.

"Well, not all the time but when it needs to get done," she said. "Anyway, you couldn't ask for a more beautiful classroom, could you?"

I looked around. The changing leaves had turned the whole world into a crazily colorful mix. It was almost too vividly red and too gold and bright green to believe. And pretty soon they'd all turn brown and drop to the ground, not caring one bit about their wasted beauty.

Nothing like Mr. James's room, when you stopped to think about it.

Mountain Laurel.

The leaves here have already changed color. They hadn't turned when I left home, had they? I don't know anymore. Maybe they have turned there now too. My grandmother waits all year until the weatherman tells her when the peak color weekend will be and then she rushes upstate and looks at the leaves.

Sometimes I just want to scream at her. Aren't they beautiful all year? What are you waiting for? Red? Green? Purple? Who cares?

What are you waiting for? What?

* * *

I only went to Debbie Sanders's funeral because
my mother made me go. She told me that if I didn't go,
I'd regret it someday. *But,* she added, it was my choice.

Yeah, right.

Of course I went, but I didn't want to and it wasn't
just because I was scared, which I was. I just didn't think
I belonged. I didn't think I knew Debbie well enough. I
hadn't even cried yet. It wasn't that I didn't like her. Or
that I didn't feel really bad. But I kept asking myself, if I
died, would I want to see Debbie Sanders at my funeral?

So why was I going?

I didn't think it would matter.

There *was* school that day, but the funeral was at one
o'clock so a lot of kids were getting picked up. The whole
day was crazy, kind of frenetic. We were in school but
we weren't. My mother said she'd pick me up in front.
Marcella was going with her mother too.

"Do you feel funny?" I asked Marcella.

"I don't know," she said, and shrugged. "No." Then,
"Yes."

We both sat on the cold floor outside the main office
where we could see our moms when they pulled up to
get us. We had our huge backpacks on our laps, waiting
with us.

"Wanna hear this weird thing?" I asked.

• 53 •

Marcella turned to look at me.

"I was in line in the cafeteria last week." As I began to talk, I was remembering it at the same time. "Debbie Sanders was a couple of people in front of me. She was with her friends. You know, Jamie and Alison."

Marcella nodded.

"But she didn't buy lunch. She just got a milk."

"So?" Marcella said.

"I heard her telling her friends she wasn't going to buy lunch all week, just milk, so she could save up her lunch money to get this CD."

I paused, thinking. Trying to figure it out. I couldn't really put what I was feeling into the right words. Why that made me so unbelievably sad. "I guess she never got to buy it."

Marcella's mother drove up in her van.

"That's my car," Marcella said, getting up.

The funeral was so crowded that there was no room inside the sanctuary. Most of the grown-ups made their way inside, including my mother. She tried to get me to come with her, but I said I wanted to stand in the lobby with the other kids from my grade and she let me.

A lot of people had to stand against the back wall, my mother told me later. There were no seats left. No space anywhere. Even more people spilled out into the waiting room. There were loudspeakers set up so everyone could hear what was being said.

By my third day at Mountain Laurel, everyone seemed pretty used to me. But just used to me enough to realize I changed the mix. We all sat in the living room. It was pretty crowded. Gretchen was the only one with an assigned seat. Her seat. A big armchair with a hard back that looked really uncomfortable. Perfect for her.

Mr. Simone was there. I figured out he usually went home at night and came back in the morning, right after breakfast. But this evening he was in the living room too, on a piano bench that had no piano. Karen was on the floor with her legs crossed. Gretchen was in her big, uncomfortable chair. Some of the younger boys were in their pajamas. It was all so weird. Like we were having some kind of little sleepover, like this was normal.

But at least it was warm. There was a fire in the fireplace. I was hoping to soak up as much of the heat as I could, maybe store it in my skin cells. I felt like I hadn't been warm since I got here. The first thing I was going to do when I got home—in two more days, but who's counting?—was take a really hot, filled-up-to-the-top bath and not care about wasting water, heating oil, or electricity. And I would wear my shoes all day, maybe even sleep in them.

"Find a seat, gentlemen. Find a seat," Gretchen was saying, waving her arms again. "And ladies." She looked at me.

John was the only kid already sitting down. It looked as though he had been there awhile. He was on the couch. He had his knees pressed together and a small rubber ball, which he started squeezing in his fist.

"Quickly, everyone," Gretchen said. "Quietly."

It took me awhile to realize that nobody but John had chosen a seat yet. They were waiting for me, for very different reasons. But in order to do so without looking obvious, everyone was shifting around the room, which was making John very upset. Drew seemed to take this as a sign and sat down on the exact far side of the same couch where John sat. His legs bounced up and down with the precision of a piston engine. Billy, still in army fatigues, took a chair by the door. He started complaining for everyone to sit down, loudly and then under his breath.

I decided to sit on the couch right in between Drew and John. It seemed a fairly safe place to be. Considering.

"Move," Tommy said. He was suddenly standing right in front of John.

It reminded me of the lunchroom at school, or the camp bus or the auditorium, or anywhere there are seats and people, and people picking where they are going to sit. Those on the upper end of the food chain get to pick where they will sit and the ones on the lower end are out of luck.

It's the same everywhere.

But John didn't budge. He acted as if he hadn't heard. So Tommy kicked him.

"Get up. I'm sitting here," Tommy said.

John looked straight ahead.

"Move, blockhead." Tommy kicked him again, this time a little harder. But John didn't budge.

"Everyone has fifteen seconds to find a seat," Gretchen announced. I knew she could see what was going on with John and Tommy, but she didn't do anything about it. She just started counting. I thought she had picked an odd number to count to. Even in preschool they usually only give you to the count of five. Ten at the most.

John started breathing really hard. And he was big, so his chest was moving way up and down.

"I will not move," John said. "This is my seat. I came down especially early. I always sit here on Wednesday nights. I have been here since . . ." John looked at his watch. It was the first movement he made. "Since seven twenty-three p.m."

Most everyone else had found somewhere to sit— the floor, a chair, or the other couch. One of the younger boys in flannel pajamas sat on the piano bench with Mr. Simone.

"Ten, eleven . . ."

John was frozen again, like a soldier. Tommy finally turned his glare over to Drew, and Drew slithered to the floor. Tommy took the recently vacated spot next to me.

"Thirteen, fourteen, fifteen." And everyone was sitting. Gretchen looked satisfied.

"It's Wednesday night," she then began. "But before we can have our regular evening reading, I want to discuss behavior for tomorrow's trip."

There was a quiet rumble of voices, but I couldn't tell if it was because this was something to look forward to or dread. Gretchen closed her mouth and waited for the quiet to return, which it promptly did.

"Mr. Simone has a list of the children he will be taking in his car. Karen has her list and Sam will be driving as well," Gretchen went on.

The name *Sam* definitely brought out a little cheer and made me wonder who he was.

"We will be leaving right after first morning period.

Maggie will pack our lunches. And remember . . ." Gretchen lifted her chin. She was almost swallowed up by that big chair but somehow her voice filled the room. The energy of twitching limbs and tapping and shifting, of being too still for too long, was held down while she talked.

"There will be no foul language. No hitting. No touching of any kind. No throwing. No rude noises, natural or otherwise. No loud voices during the car ride. Respect yourself and respect one another."

I got the feeling that for every forbidden act there had been a lewd or indecent incident that everyone in this room knew about but me. Gretchen was winding down. I could tell she was tired. A long day? Old age? Or simply the expenditure of all the energy required to be a mean bitch? Gretchen rested for a minute.

But no one moved. Not yet.

"Is that understood by all?" Gretchen then finished.

All the boys nodded with varying degrees of enthusiasm or sarcasm, but Gretchen waited until everyone had shown her, one by one, that he had heard. I noticed that she allowed for a certain degree of extraneous noise during this accounting.

"And now, can we begin," Gretchen said, because it wasn't a question. She opened the book on her lap and then, in an apparent change of mind, passed the book to Mr. Simone. I watched him take a breath, about to start.

"Where are we going?" I heard my voice.

I looked around. When the attention focused on me, the room got still. Even the twitching and shifting stopped. Only John was still squeezing his rubber ball. And now that it was quiet in the room, I could actually hear the air going in and out, like a respirator.

Some of the boys giggled, and I knew Gretchen wouldn't like that. She was so serious. This was probably a trip to some government building to watch how they make postage stamps, or worse, one of those simulated pioneer villages where all the people working there act like they never saw a Game Boy before. Or one of those museums with life-size statues showing daily existence in prehistoric times, and all the boys would go nuts over the models of cavewomen without their shirts on.

"We are going bowling," Gretchen said finally.

Night was the hardest. That night, again it felt like I was alone in the world and nothing was all right.

There was a little table lamp in my room but I couldn't reach it from the bed. If I wanted to leave it on and read or look at a magazine, I'd have to get up and walk across the freezing-cold floor when I was ready to go to sleep. I had to keep telling myself that it would be better in the morning.

That a person can tolerate anything, as long as they know it's going to end.

And this was going to end soon. A couple more days. Think of the people in this world who had it so much worse than I did. There were plane crashes, and cancer, and the Holocaust.

I thought about all that for a while until I was so frightened I couldn't move.

The moonlight came right into the room and spread across the wood floor like a luminous blanket. It made the room seem bigger and scarier and kind of lopsided. Or maybe it *was* lopsided. The floorboards were so old and rickety. I think the whole room slanted to the right.

I yanked the covers loose from the bottom of the bed so that I could sit up to look out the window and still pull the blanket up to my face.

There he was. I put my hand up to the window at the same time he did. I could barely make out his figure but I was sure it was Drew. He waved his hand back and forth and then he was gone.

I dreamed that night that I was dreaming. In my dream I woke up and thought I was home, but I wasn't.

It was like a cruel trick my mind had played on me. It was part feeling, part sound, part sight, part words. Partly real. Partly not.

A dream like a nightmare.

Like a Mountain Laurel field trip.

Billy, it turned out, was an excellent bowler,

which was a good thing because he kept telling us how awesome he was the whole ride over in Sam's pickup. Sam was the Mountain Laurel handyman, I learned. Billy told me Sam did pretty much everything. He was also the one who worked all day with Angel no matter what he was doing, which explained why Angel was never in class. So whether Sam was fixing one of Gretchen's cars or building a greenhouse or putting up deer fencing, Angel was doing it too.

Except bowling, apparently. Angel was in Karen's car with Carl and Drew and two other boys. Mr. Simone got one more, plus Tommy and John.

I'm guessing Mr. Simone didn't have kids. Or he didn't have boys. Or he just hadn't been teaching very long because even *I* knew it was a big mistake when he directed Tommy over to the lanes to plug everyone's name into the bowling-computer-console thing while Mr. Simone stood in line for shoes. We had two lanes. We were supposed to have one with bumpers, but it didn't work out that way.

Karen was talking to the manager about that.

Sam was in the bathroom running cold water over Drew's fingers. Drew had already smashed his hand between two balls when he was trying to pick one from the rack. Tommy sat at the console typing furiously and laughing.

"That's stupid," I said to Tommy. I was sitting in one of the molded plastic seats around the scorekeeper's station, or whatever it's called.

"What?" Tommy answered as if "what" were an answer.

We both looked up at the wide screen, where an interesting X-rated version of everyone's name was lit up in green.

"Putting those kinds of words up there," I said. "They're just going to reset the whole thing and you won't get to play. So why do it?"

Tommy looked at me like I was some kind of an idiot.

Carl thought it was hilarious, though. So did Billy. But not Mr. Simone, who had lost all his sense of humor—he had very little to begin with—at the bowling-shoe counter. He didn't appreciate having to go back to the counter and ask the guy with the seventy bazillion tattoos to reset the computer. Tommy had to sit out the first round of bowling.

But it wasn't until the boy who unstuck stuck balls from the gutter came over to our lane for the fifth time that I started to wonder how this must all look to an outsider. He was a skinny kid with the butt of his blue jeans nearing the back of his knees. That was mostly all I got to see of him as he walked down the raised rim between the lanes and gave the ball a little push. This sent the ball straight into the black hole of the unknown where it would somehow pop back up into the console thingy where, of course, Mr. Simone now sat in control.

"Aw, give me another chance," Billy called out to the boy with the baggy jeans.

The boy turned and looked up at Billy. "Huh?"

"Can you roll it back this way instead?" Billy said. "I don't want a gutter ball."

"Nobody does," the kid said, but he lifted the purple marbleized ball out of the gutter and gave it a push toward Billy.

"Thanks," Billy said, waving.

The boy hiked up his jeans and started walking back. Maybe he didn't notice anything. It was just another night at the bowling alley and we were just another bunch of bad bowlers.

Billy bowled a 145. Tommy got an 80, mostly because he kept spinning around like Fred Flintstone and shouting "Yabba dabba doo" and then losing his ball in the next person's lane. I got a 95, because I really stink. Drew bowled a 40 because he could barely lift the smallest ball we could find for him, even after his fingers felt better.

Carl refused to finish after he sat on a hot dog and spent the last hour with his back to the wall, hiding the mustard stain on his ass.

John didn't play at all, because the little vent on the side of the ball return that blows air wasn't working and he couldn't dry his hands and Karen wouldn't let him switch to the other lane.

No, nobody wants a gutter ball.

I didn't make my bed Friday morning because I was leaving. I had one knee on my bed and I was looking out the window. I had my coat and hat on. I knew that upstairs in the House all the boys were stripping their beds and washing up. Getting ready to leave for the weekend.

I could watch for my mother's car and watch what was going on with everyone else at the same time. My mom would come, I figured, because my dad had brought me. I was entertaining myself with thoughts of how distant I would act when she got here. I let the time pass with various daydreams of how I would get her to feel guilty. I was so deeply involved in my different scenarios, I let my eyes lock into a blurry stare until I could no longer see outside the window to the chairs and the ground and the house below, but I saw myself in the window's reflection.

I look like my father. And Cecily looks like our mom. Someone once told us that the first child always looks like the father on the outside but is more like the mother on the inside. And the second child is the opposite. It's some kind of bioenergetic theory. But it seems to hold true with us Singers since I have my dad's dark hair and tall body while Cecily is lighter in color and more *petite*, as my mom likes to say. It was sort of our family joke or family teasing—whenever one of us was a little too emotional or excitable or didn't think before they said something, that was our mom's trait. That was me.

And if someone was a little too critical or withdrawn, that was more like Cecily and our dad.

So for the longest time I remember thinking I didn't have a choice. I have straight, dark hair. I was born that way. I have long toes, with the second toe stretching out past my big toe. So does my dad. I was born that way. And I was always the too-sensitive one.

Cecily was the rational one, the one you want next to you in battle. She was only eight but Cecily was the one who made the obligatory call to Grandma because she knew it was the right thing to do. I was the one who stomped off when we decided to go to the Outback instead of the Olive Garden. (God, what was the matter with me?) I was too dramatic. Overwrought. I was born that way. I was the crazy one.

Of course, they always change it when it fits their needs. I had my dad's brains. But of course, so did Cecily. Our dad was the Ivy Leaguer. (We even know his SAT scores.) I had my mom's athletic grace but my dad's hand-eye coordination. (A volleyball scholarship looming.) My mom's vision, because I didn't need glasses, but my dad's hearing, because he didn't listen either.

I don't know.

But lately, I just wanted to be me.

I still hadn't seen my mom's car pull up. I didn't see Drew at the window, either. He must have been getting ready for the weekend. Friday-morning chores included stripping the beds and cleaning bathrooms. There was a cleaning woman who came once a week and cleaned the whole house but, Drew told me, she refused to clean the upstairs toilets.

I was still kneeling on my unmade bed when Karen knocked, sort of, and then walked in.

"You've got to strip your bed, Mia," she said. "C'mon; it's late."

Karen was dressed; looked like she was heading out. Then she stopped and looked at my suitcase and my coat.

"Mia, do you think you're going home?" she said.

I remember, I think I remember, saying yes.

"Mia, it's a Mountain Laurel rule. The first month. No weekends home until one month. You must have known that. Didn't you know that?"

"What?" I said. I think I even turned around and

looked behind me, as if she must have been talking to someone else. "What?"

That's all I remember before I went crazy.

I found out Mountain Laurel wasn't like *A Beautiful Mind* or *Girl, Interrupted*, *I Never Promised You a Rose Garden*, or even *One Flew over the Cuckoo's Nest*. Or any of those movies about crazy people and crazy places.

There were no drugs. No needles. No bed straps. No big men in white coats.

There was just Gretchen.

It took Gretchen a really long time to make her way out of her house, across the lawn, and up the steep stairs of the nursery school and into my room. I even saw, through the window by my bed, Gretchen pause and stoop down to pet her big, husky dog. Like she had all the time in the world.

Karen told me I could stay in my room the rest of the morning if I wanted. But she didn't say it mean or angry, the way that sounds. She really meant it. She said if I needed to just be away from things for a while, she understood. She said she'd save me breakfast and she left.

About an hour and a half later Gretchen came into my room. She stood in the doorway.

"Mia, get up now. It's time," she said to me.

"I don't want to." I was back under my covers with all my clothes on. My shoes on.

"We often do things we don't want to do," Gretchen said. "That's life."

I hate the *That's life* explanation. It's right up there with *Because I said so*. And my all-time favorite, *Not everything's fair*.

Then Gretchen walked all the way into the room. She sat on the end of the bed.

"Mia, you're going to be all right. But right now, all you have to work on is getting out of this bed and coming in for lunch."

Then Gretchen stood up. With a lot of effort, she went slowly down the stairs and across the frozen lawn and back into her house.

My mother doesn't believe me, but I can remember lots of things from before Cecily was born. I can remember when it was just me. I can't remember my dad from then, at least not very well, but I can remember when it was just me and my mom.

We were hiking at the nature center. I must have been about four years old. I can see it all perfectly, and I know I've been back there since, but that doesn't explain why I remember that day so well. It was fall, early fall, and still hot. I was in shorts and my mother had this big, huge dress on. She was pregnant. Cecily was born in October, so she must have been pretty far along. But I don't remember her big and fat. To me my mother was always beautiful.

We walked along the trail really slowly. Like there was nothing we had to do. Nowhere we had to be. It was long before elementary school, even before Tumble Bugs Academy or the Music for Kiddies classes. It was hundreds of years before homework and grades and standardized tests.

Before I could even have dreamed of a place like Mountain Laurel.

My mother says I couldn't possibly remember that day, but I do. We stopped at every trail marker. I would run ahead to read the number even though I couldn't read. I would just say anything, any number that popped into my head, and my mother would agree. Even though I knew I wasn't *really* reading, pleasing her made me feel good. I remember that clearly.

The water was low in the stream that ran under the wooden bridge, but we sat and dangled our legs over the edge and watched the bugs flying low over the mud. Then we got up, but only when *I* said I wanted to. We took the longer fork in the trail that day, the left fork that we had never taken before—the Lollipop Trail.

I was on a field trip years and years later when I found out that *lollipop* referred to the shape of the trail. The first part of the trail was one long straight walk— the stick. Then it looped around in a big circle—the candy part. But back then, that day with my mom, I thought it meant there were lollipops to be found.

Lollipops! Maybe on the ground or hanging from the trees. Lollipops. Maybe they would be just lying along the side of the narrow dirt trail. I never questioned it, so I never asked. I just kept my eyes open and for the longest time I assumed we were both looking for the same thing.

"I'm really sorry," Drew told me.

"What for?" I said.

"I'm going soon. My dad is coming to pick me up. I'm sorry you have to stay. I heard."

"Heard what?"

"I heard you crying."

"I wasn't crying," I said, because I hadn't been. "I never cry."

"Never?" He looked at me.

I smiled at Drew because he looked sadder than I did.

I had been sitting by the beach, freezing, although the sun was strong and warm. I came down here right after that warm and fuzzy visit from Gretchen, after I ate the breakfast that Karen had saved for me. I didn't want to watch everyone else going home. There was a wooden dock left in the middle of the roped-off swimming area of the pond. It rocked slowly with the wind; otherwise everything was still.

"That's okay, Drew," I said. "It can't be that bad here over the weekend. Hey, it can't be worse." I surprised myself; I laughed.

"It's not," Drew said. He sat down beside me.

"Have you ever stayed over the weekend?" I asked.

"Once. When I first got here. There's a one-month rule or something like that."

"Yeah, I know. I guess it's like at camp when they

won't let you call your mother for the first two weeks, no matter how homesick you are."

"They do that?"

I could tell Drew had never been to sleep-away camp, and all of a sudden it seemed like a ludicrous comparison anyway.

"Never mind."

We both stared out at the water. Again, I noticed all the tall pine trees on the far side. So perfectly aligned. Someone had made a forest. Pine needles covered the entire hillside, an amber carpet, almost perfect.

"They let you watch TV," Drew told me. "On weekends."

"Yeah?"

"Yeah, and you don't have to eat in the dining room. You eat in the kitchen. It's warmer in there."

"Does Gretchen let you keep your shoes on?"

"No, not that I've heard." Drew lowered his head as if he had disappointed me.

"Hey, it's not your fault."

"Tommy told me once they went to the movies in town," Drew went on. His fingers moved constantly while he was talking. He had shifted closer to me until he was touching the hem of my coat.

"What movie did they see?"

"I don't know," he said. I don't think Drew noticed, but he was running the fringe of my scarf through his fingers while he talked.

We both heard a car beeping. It sounded far away. The dip down toward the water muffled any sound and you couldn't see the House or the barn or the nursery school from here.

"Is that for you?" I asked.

He nodded. "Maybe," Drew said. But he didn't move. He was still touching my scarf, gently.

"Is it your dad?"

"I guess so," Drew said. "Will you be here when I get back?"

"Right here," I told him.

Only then did Drew stand up. He seemed content and took off running. He shouted good-bye just before he made it over the crest of the hill, and he was gone.

Mountain Laurel.
I hate it here. I can't remember the last time I felt so homesick. Sleep-away camp, maybe. No, this is worse. No comparison. Camp was hot.
Here it's freezing.

* * *

I had gone to camp every summer since third grade. And they really *don't* let you call your mom. It was funny, because a lot of kids from my town went to sleep-away camp. It was like the thing to do. Parents started talking about it in January. I could tell some camps were better than others, but I could never tell which were the better ones and which weren't. They were all really expensive.

All I know is that even moms who were completely overprotective (like mine), even moms who wouldn't let their kids sleep at someone's house because that family watched TV on school nights, sent their kids to sleep-away camp. Moms who sent their kids to school with soy milk, moms who kept their kids in car seats until they were seven—they all sent their kids to sleep-away camp.

I always thought the joke was on them because everything happens at camp. Everything.

Lying.

Stealing.

Sneaking out.

Food fights.

Shaving.

Piercing.

Kissing.

It hadn't happened again since, but I was kissed at

sleep-away camp two years ago by a boy named Jared Job. (That was really his name.)

Jared's sister Jenna was my best camp friend and bunk mate. They also had a younger sister, Joely, who went to the day camp. They were all nicknamed Jay Jay. Get it? Oh, brother.

It was the last day of camp. Everyone had their stuff all packed, sleeping bags rolled and bunks swept clean. Most everyone was milling around the mess hall waiting for the bus or for their parents to come and get them. That's when Jenna told me her brother liked me. She had a note from him, folded into a tiny tight square.

"He likes you," Jenna told me.

"I don't even know him," I answered.

"You've known him as long as you've known me."

That was true. Jenna was a year younger than me but she was in the same grade and we were in the same bunk. We met two weeks before, on our first night when we both wanted to go to sleep but the other girls in our bunk were talking and playing music. At the same time we both went outside to complain to our senior counselor, Melinda. Jenna and I had an instant nerd bonding. And we were best friends by morning.

It happens like that at camp. Every microcosm of time takes on greater meaning.

A whole year can be squished down into a week. An hour into a minute. Because at camp, time is measured out for you right from the start. Before you even get there you know you have only two weeks. Or one month. Maybe two. It's like having a terminal illness.

I unwrapped my tiny square note. It said:

Do you like me?
Yes or No.
Circle one.

Jenna was looking on, waiting.

"Are you sure this is from your brother?" I asked.

Jenna assured me she had seen him write it and fold it up, with instructions to give it to me, and depending on my answer, I was to meet Jared in bunk number five in ten minutes.

Microcosms.

Ten minutes later, I was making out with Jared Job for no other reason than he said he liked me.

He was nice enough. He asked me if he could kiss me after he read my response.

Do you like me?

I had circled *Yes*.

We pressed our lips together and kept them there for

nearly twenty-five minutes, barely moving. I felt absolutely nothing. Except the sharp metal of my braces digging into the soft flesh inside my lips.

Mountain Laurel was different on the weekend, completely different. It was more about who didn't get to go home rather than who did.

Billy went home. Carl and Tommy went home. So did some of the other kids — I still got their names mixed up. Drew went home. Angel, that boy who never comes to class, stayed, except he spent all of his time somewhere with Sam. And when he did come into the House for dinner or lunch he wore a tool belt, exactly like Sam's. It had hammers and a screwdriver hanging from it. Gretchen made him take it off and hang it in the mudroom every time. And every time he'd walk in with it again, just so everyone would see it, and she'd make him hang it up again.

John stayed that weekend, but I got the feeling he didn't always stay. He kept asking Gretchen questions about what was expected of him on weekends. What time would dinner be? What time was bedtime? Where could he go? What would he do? Where did Sam live? Where did Maggie go? Where did Mr. Simone go? Did Mr. Simone watch *20/20*, because he said he did.

Then Saturday morning, John asked me when my birthday was.

I answered, "May eighteenth."

There didn't seem any harm in answering, although I couldn't think of a reason why he would ask me that. I kept looking toward the door, hoping someone else would walk in. I didn't want to be alone in the room with him. We were both standing on the same side of the long table. I wished I was nearer to the door.

"May eighteenth," John repeated. He straightened his back and his eyes kind of shifted back and forth. He never looked directly at you.

"Perry Como. Czar Nicholas the Second. Margot Fonteyn. Frank Capra. That's all I can think of."

"What?" I asked.

"They were also born on May eighteenth. And Reggie Jackson."

I didn't know who Perry Como was or Frank Capra or Margot whatever, but I had heard of Nicholas II of Russia from social studies. And Reggie Jackson was a baseball player, I think.

"Really?" I had to strain my neck to look up at him and smile. The other boys teased him constantly, and I always thought if only John knew his own size it would all be over in a matter of seconds. He could probably have squeezed the life out of either Tommy or Carl without breaking a sweat.

"My birthday is September twenty-first." John then proceeded to list famous people who shared his birthday. "Stephen King, the author of *Carrie* and *The Shining*. Faith Hill and Ricki Lake. Bill Murray, comedian and star of such films as *Ghostbusters*, *Stripes*, *Groundhog Day*. H. G. Wells, the author of *The Time Machine*, *The Invisible Man*, and *The War of the Worlds*, was born on September twenty-first. And Chuck Jones, who you may not have heard of, but he was the creator of Bugs Bunny."

I was just speechless.

"You know who Bugs Bunny is, don't you?"

I nodded, and that's when I understood what the other boys at Mountain Laurel had figured out and why, despite his size, no one was afraid of him. John was harmless. He was just a little boy. Sure, a weird little boy. In a big huge body.

"He's doing it again, Mr. Simone," Tommy was shouting.

Four boys were sitting at a table in the corner. John was one of them. Drew was another, and one of the younger boys, Sebastian. Tommy was the fourth. Carl had already been told to stay away from Tommy, so he was sitting at a table near Mr. Simone, playing with blocks. Angel hadn't come at all. There was one other boy who always seemed to be there at the beginning of class but never at the end. I never found out his name.

Everyone came back Sunday. It was total bedlam for the next few hours, through dinner and the rest of the evening. But by Monday morning everything was pretty much back to normal, Mountain Laurel style. Math Experience was scheduled.

Drew, Tommy, Sebastian, and John were supposed to be playing cards—poker, in fact, which I suppose is how they were experiencing math. I actually had a math workbook and I was drawing pictures in it.

"Just ignore him, Tommy," Mr. Simone responded from the other side of the room, where Carl was clearly upset about something. I think Mr. Simone went to the Don't-Ask-Don't-Tell School of Education, where I think I can say most all of my teachers from second grade on had been trained.

"God, John, what's your freakin' problem?" Tommy was saying loudly. Mr. Simone didn't even look up.

But I did.

John was sitting straight in his chair, then all of a sudden just leaned over, kind of stuck his nose under the table, and took a deep breath. It was an odd and completely obvious gesture, but John didn't seem to understand that other people could see him and were, at this point, watching him closely. For a few minutes it was more or less peaceful, and then John repeated the same duck-and-sniff action.

This time, Tommy jumped up from the table. "Jesus! He did it again. He's smelling his farts. Goddammit, I'm outta here."

And that was that.

Class was over. Mr. Simone had lost all hope of regaining the control he never had.

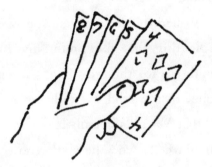

Marcella Campbell had been my best friend since preschool. My parents and her parents were also friends, especially her mom and my mom. When we were little, that worked out great. We spent practically every day together.

I knew that Marcella's mom and my mom talked during the day when we were at school, or when we were playing or in our rooms, but somehow it never occurred to me that they talked about us. But as we got older and ended up in different classes and with different teachers and then finally in different levels of math and English, it became abundantly clear what they were talking about.

And it became clear, at least to me, that they were competing. At first Mom and I were the clear winners. I was cocaptain of the middle-school track team. I was president of my sixth-grade class. I was in pre-algebra, while Marcella was only in M6. And twice a week, I was pulled out for Junior Great Books. Marcella was not.

I always had this feeling that in a way my mom was secretly gloating, that in her mind my "higher" achievements made up for the fact that Marcella's family had more money than we did. We didn't even have the "kind" of money that Marcella's family had, whatever that meant.

Then Marcella won the sixth-grade geography bee and she qualified for the schoolwide finals. If she won, she would go on to the states. Either way, win or lose, her name went on a plaque by the front office.

"I just guessed," Marcella told me. She was at my house after school. The finals were in two days.

"You what?"

"On every single question. I just guessed. You know, I don't know anything about geography. I don't even know the United States. Remember, in fourth grade? Remember that test when you have to fill in all the states?"

I nodded. It seemed like so long ago. Even then, I had stayed up in bed filling in blank map after map. The teacher had given us all one practice map but my mother had gone to the library to use the copy machine. She made me ten blank maps and I filled in every one. I got 100.

Marcella got an 85.

"I remember," I said.

"Well. So?" Marcella said. We were both lying on the rug on my floor, looking up.

"Well, so, what?"

"Well, so, I didn't just turn into some world geography wiz in the last two years. I guessed. On every single one. I swear to God. I didn't know one single answer." Marcella sat up.

I sat up too. I thought a minute and then said, "Well, that's even better. It's great. You won for the sixth grade and you get your name on the wall. Forever."

"It's not great. I have to take the schoolwide. It was just luck. It won't happen again. I'll get a terrible grade. I'll look like an idiot."

"No one will know," I said.

"My parents are so proud of me," Marcella said. She had long, silky black hair and big dark eyes. She had thick eyebrows, too. My mother used to say Marcella was exotic looking and one day she was going to be a beautiful woman. But in middle school she was just kind of different, and that never went over too well.

Right now, she looked like she was going to cry.

"They never expect a sixth grader to win," I tried. "It's always an eighth grader."

"Marc Weinroth was in seventh," Marcella said.

"You're in sixth."

"It's a bee, you know. It's oral. It's out loud or whatever. Everybody will be watching. And I won't answer one single question."

"You could study?" I tried some more.

Marcella looked at me. "I can't study the whole world."

We both lay back down to rest our backs and our brains. We were quiet. I didn't envy Marcella. In fact, I was glad it wasn't me. I was so glad.

"You could be sick," I said after a few minutes.

"What?" Marcella sat up again.

"You could be sick in two days."

"Or I could try to study a little," she said quietly.

"Or you could be sick."

"Maybe I could just try the Unites States and South

America. At least, just that."

"Yeah," I said. "You could."

Marcella studied a lot, I think. Her father came home early from work two nights in a row and helped her. Her mother went out and bought Marcella a computer game where you are a detective going around the world, from country to country, trying to catch some cartoon thief.

And then Friday, she got sick and missed the schoolwide geography bee anyway. The sixth-grade runner-up, Max Pachman, took Marcella's place at the last minute.

You really can't study the whole world.

I heard my mother on the phone with Marcella's mother that evening after the geography bee. She was so sorry and she was so certain Marcella would have done great. And don't worry, there's another geography bee next year. Think how much better Marcella will do when she's in seventh grade.

But I couldn't help feeling my mother was relieved. She was relieved it wasn't *me* who had disappointed *her* in front of the whole world. I could just hear it in her voice.

And I couldn't help imagining that when I went to Mountain Laurel that Marcella's mother was at home thinking to herself: *That would never be* my *daughter.*

I imagined Mrs. Campbell silently shaking her head in disbelief while consoling my mother and saying it was all going to work out. Walking around her cherrywood and granite kitchen with its subzero appliances, saying, "Everything is going to be fine."

All the while, she would be just so glad it wasn't Marcella.

Carl and Tommy got caught smoking. Mr. Simone brought them into the House, where I was supposed to be reading with Karen. It was my language arts time. I *was* reading, and so was Karen. She was sitting on the couch by the fireplace with her feet up, shoes off, of course, and I was stretched out on the floor by the rug.

Then Carl and Tommy burst in and the cold air from outside clung to them. For a long while the chill seemed to lift from their hair and their clothing and fill the air. Gretchen made her way into the living room and sat down slowly in her armchair. Karen didn't even stop reading.

"So what is this?" Gretchen asked. She held a half-burned cigarette in her fingers. She held it in the air briefly, inspecting it as if she really didn't know what it was, and then let her arm down.

"I don't know," Carl started.

"It's not ours," Tommy said. They both stood before her. Tommy, thin and tall, had his arms crossed in front of him. Carl had on a beanie hat, pulled down nearly to his eyes. He shifted his weight back and forth, from one leg to the other. Tommy had some unusual facial tics that seemed to act up under stress.

"Mr. Simone says he saw you two smoking behind the barn and when you ran away he found this where you were standing," Gretchen said. "It was still glowing when he picked it up."

Her accent was so clear and deliberate when she spoke slowly. She would have been a good interrogator, I thought. She is mean enough. In fact, she reminded me of those war movies where the enemy officer tries to get the captured resistance fighter to betray his friends.

Maybe beat the soles of their feet or force slivers of wood up their fingernails. I sat up and leaned back against the couch where Karen was still reading.

"Well, it's not mine," Tommy repeated. I thought he was going to need something a lot better than that.

"Mr. Simone saw smoke coming out of your mouths. He saw you smoking. He found your cigarette," Gretchen listed. Mr. Simone nodded.

"Smoke coming out of our mouths?" Tommy said.

"Yes, Tommy. That is correct," Gretchen said.

I shook my head. *She won't even need slivers of wood*, I thought.

It was quiet and then Carl said suddenly, "It's the cold."

"Excuse me?"

"It's cold out. Everybody has smoke coming out of their mouths." And with that, Carl just darted right out of the living room and we all heard the front door bang shut. Karen put down her book. Carl must have run around the side of the house. He popped up by the living-room window. He rapped on the glass and then started puffing. And pointing. And puffing and pointing. Tommy finally caught on.

"It's the cold," Tommy said suddenly. "See the smoke?"

He looked at Mr. Simone for a response and then

everyone turned to Gretchen. Carl came running back inside; another rush of cold followed him.

"So you are telling me that you were not smoking," Gretchen continued, seemingly unimpressed.

Both of the boys nodded.

"That it was the natural moisture in your warm breath forming condensation in the cold air, which Mr. Simone mistakenly confused as smoking?" Gretchen said. The boys nodded happily.

Mr. Simone stepped forward as if he had something to say about that, but Gretchen raised her hand like a traffic cop.

Tommy and Carl looked at each other and then smiled. "Yup," they both said.

The fireplace crackled. Gretchen leaned forward in her chair, which was really so much bigger than she was. She lowered her voice.

"Do you think it is really very important to me that you were smoking a cigarette?" she asked. "Do you think you are the first or will be the last teenage boys to think smoking a cigarette is a cool thing to do?"

Tommy and Carl looked confused about how exactly to answer that. In normal circumstances it would be advisable not to answer, but this was Gretchen, and not answering was not an option.

"No," Tommy started slowly.

"Uh, no," Carl agreed.

Gretchen leaned back again. She pulled her sweater around her. She closed her eyes a moment, but everyone knew she wasn't done. When she opened them again, she began. "But to throw a lit cigarette into a ravine of dry leaves. Next to a barn." She took a breath. She shook her head as if she was thinking of the possibilities. "Next to my barn."

Carl and Tommy both dropped their eyes. They knew they were finished.

"My husband built that barn," Gretchen went on. "Many years ago."

I had never heard Gretchen or anyone speak about a husband. I hadn't seen anyone who might be a husband. The only men at Mountain Laurel were Sam and Mr. Simone. It was hard to imagine Gretchen as someone who had ever been young, let alone married and in love. Harder to imagine someone in love with *her*. But I guess she was, and I guess whoever had built this whole place and even planted those pine trees up on the hill had done it with love. Gretchen and her husband had probably dreamed of watching the saplings grow into a forest. Maybe they dreamed of growing old together and sitting in this living room, just the two of them, with the fire keeping them warm.

I looked around the room. But it sure didn't turn out that way, did it?

"Never," Gretchen said suddenly. "Never again will you be so thoughtless and selfish as to jeopardize this land or this house or anything or anyone here. If you want to smoke, smoke. I can't stop you, either of you. Nobody can stop you if you want to continue such a dirty, foolish habit. It will be your choice. But not here. Not in my house."

Gretchen stood up. She looked tired. As soon as she left the room, Carl and Tommy took off. Mr. Simone let out a deep breath. He nodded to Karen, who simply nodded back, and then he left as well.

"Did Gretchen's husband die?"

Karen and I were peeling carrots. Gretchen said everyone at Mountain Laurel was expected to contribute by way of regular chores and duties, but I had a feeling she had just made that up on the spot. Gretchen was real good at coming up with longtime rules and procedures whenever anyone looked like they were wandering, even for a second.

I suppose I had been wandering. The next thing I knew I was peeling carrots with Karen. Maggie had left a list of predinner preparations.

"Yes," Karen answered. "Just a couple of years ago. They were married forty-nine years and were still in love. It was very sad."

It was hard for me to feel anything right then. I couldn't get the image of a bossy, cranky old woman out of my mind. Maybe his death had changed her. Maybe she had once been more *lovable*.

"He was the complete opposite of Gretchen," Karen went on. "He was silly and easygoing. He was always making jokes that made Gretchen laugh when she didn't want to."

Guess not.

"I cared for him very deeply. After I got divorced, Gretchen and Peter became family to me. They offered me a job and a place to live. I've been teaching here ever since."

"When was that?" I asked.

Karen stopped what she was doing to answer me. She put down her knife. So I stopped to listen.

"Seventeen years ago," Karen said after a while, as if she had just calculated the years and suddenly felt the passing of every one of them. "It's been seventeen years."

I wondered if she was happy or miserable. Why hadn't she married again? Did she have any children? I had this funny sense that Karen hadn't planned on staying here this long, that maybe it was like waking up from a dream only to find you're still dreaming.

Mountain Laurel
Sometimes I try to imagine where
I will be in seventeen years, or
twenty years, or five years. or shit,
next year.
 And I wonder. It scares me. I just
wonder.

After she died, I still had to pass Debbie Sanders's house every day coming home from school. I had to imagine her family inside. And I'd imagine her room, even though I had never been in it. I imagined it empty but everything left just the way it was. Maybe her clothes still lying on the floor and her notebooks open on her desk.

I don't know why. I really didn't know anything about her. I knew she had an older brother and a sister in college; that's all. I'm sure they never imagined anything like this. Or even if they imagined it, they never thought it could really happen. I didn't think I had any right to be sad or to cry when I saw her house and thought about her family inside.

But that didn't stop some other kids.

There were kids in school who thought nothing of writing something at the top of their test when they hadn't studied, like "Need a re-test. Too upset . . ." And then in little letters underneath ". . . about Debbie Sanders."

Or when they didn't have their report done or their project completed.

"Can't concentrate since the funeral."

Girls hung out, putting on makeup in the bathrooms, and when they were late for class they'd say, "We just started talking . . . about Debbie."

Sometimes, they'd cry.

I knew for a fact that those two girls in the bathroom wouldn't have been able to pick Debbie's picture out of the yearbook.

I had talked to Debbie before. She rode my bus. We were both on the volleyball team.

And still I hadn't cried at all.

Billy wasn't so bad once you got to know him a little. Once you got past the fact that he wore some article of army clothing every day, whether it was army fatigue pants or a camouflage jacket or a camouflage T-shirt. Once you stopped noticing how he bit his nails and when his nails were too short he started in on the skin of his palms until they were red and scabby.

Once you got to know him and got past all that, you liked him anyway.

He was really just a big crybaby.

Tuesday morning, my second week at Mountain Laurel, Billy burned himself on his electric blanket. Sam had to drive him to the local hospital. Any break in the routine at Mountain Laurel was a good reason to hang around and talk. Even the teachers thought so. We had hot chocolate and worked in our journals all morning.

When Billy returned he was a hero, with an ugly burn on his forearm to prove it.

"Where did you get an electric blanket, anyway?" Tommy asked him.

"None of your business," Billy answered. He had his sleeve pushed up to the top of his white chubby arm. His burn was uncovered, but it had a layer of something gooey over it. It was red and blistery and just gross enough for everyone to be interested in it.

"How did it happen?" Drew wanted to know.

"I don't know," Billy told us. "I didn't even wake up, I guess."

We were in the living room. Maggie was in the kitchen, getting lunch ready. Gretchen was on the phone with someone at Billy's house. She was in her office with the door shut. You could hear her voice, but you couldn't make out what she was saying. Billy could have called home himself, but he seemed to prefer showing us his wound.

"What a jerk you are then," Carl said. "How could you not wake up when your arm was on fire?"

"It wasn't on fire," Billy said. For this much attention, he didn't even mind being called a jerk. "The guy at the hospital said I must have been leaning on the thermostat thingy. It's a second-degree burn."

"Does it hurt?" I asked Billy. It looked like it hurt.

"Ye-ah. It hurts like hell," Billy said proudly.

The only person who wasn't interested in Billy's disgusting burn was John. John seemed to have something else on his mind entirely. He kept walking into the kitchen and talking to Maggie and then coming back out, sitting down at the table and writing in his journal.

"I'm probably going to have a scar," Billy told everyone. He was starting to lose his audience. I decided to get up and see if I could help Maggie with anything.

"If it starts to puss up," Billy was saying, "I have this yellow, sticky medicine to put on it."

Until only Drew was still listening.

"What are we having for dinner Thursday?" John was

standing in the kitchen talking to Maggie when I walked in.

"Pot roast and green beans," she told him. "Oh, hello there, Mia."

John looked at me and then hurried away. He was guilty of something. I could recognize it.

Mountain Laurel.

Sam had dinner with us tonight and he talked about this doctor, Elizabeth Kübler-Ross, who he said was really into death and dying, which sounds morbid but the way he talked about it, it wasn't. She was trying to help people deal with stuff. Anyway, Dr. Ross said everyone went through these five stages whether they were dying or knew someone who was.

Sam said Dr. Ross had the stages all mapped out and named. She said they were denial, anger, bargaining, depression, and acceptance. So I starting thinking about that.

Denial.

Anger.

Bargaining.

Depression.

Acceptance.

And it's funny. That's just what happened to me. When I got caught shoplifting.

Exactly.

The first thing I thought when the woman in Kohl's grabbed my arm was: *This can't be happening. This woman must think I'm someone else. Her daughter maybe.* Or she thought *I* worked here and she was looking for the aisle where they sell throw rugs and bathroom scales.

"You need to come to the back of the store with me," she said. "So we can talk in private." She had let go of my arm, and I was able to calm down enough to see who she was.

She looked just like any woman who would be shopping that day.

Why was this woman grabbing my arm?

She didn't have on a red apron with the name of the store printed across the front, like the other people who worked there. She had her coat on. She was even carrying a shopping bag from one of the other stores in the mall. And her pocketbook. If this woman worked here, she wouldn't be carrying a pocketbook. She looked like a mom. I remembered her now; I had noticed she was looking through the bin of little-boy socks like she wanted to buy them.

No, she couldn't be a security woman and I couldn't have just been caught shoplifting.

This was my first thought—*No way.*

Then I realized she must be undercover, looking like a regular shopper on purpose. Trying to blend in. That wasn't fair. It was a setup. A trick.

For a second that thought made me mad enough to say, "I didn't do anything."

"Maybe you didn't," the woman said. "But we need to go in the back and work it out. You haven't left the store yet. You can just come with me and no one will notice. We can talk there."

I turned around. There was a mom and her teenage

daughter a couple of racks away, definitely looking my way. And there was a boy walking by with his head turned toward me.

"What if I just put it back?" I said. I suddenly felt my heart, which had been beating so hard since I first put the gloves and belt into my bag. Now there was no stopping the pain of my heart working overtime. I couldn't think straight. My fear was taking my breath away and I couldn't breathe at all. I had to do something. I could fix this if I tried, couldn't I?

"What if I put it back right where I got it?" I tried again to bargain.

"You don't have to do that," the woman said. She had a nice voice. "I can take care of that. But we still need to talk. Back here." She was leading me again and this time I followed.

It felt like the longest walk I had ever taken anywhere. The horrible fluorescent lights buzzed overhead. The carpet made my footsteps sound heavy. We passed all the tagged and hanging clothing and all the people innocently shopping, and I had never felt more sad in my whole life. I wanted to cry so badly. It seemed like I had done the stupidest thing in the whole world and for no reason. No reason at all.

And it occurred to me right then that that had been

the point all along, hadn't it? If you take things you don't really want, don't even care about, then nothing matters. It doesn't matter if you get it, it doesn't matter if you don't. Not caring is a very powerful thing.

But I did care, didn't I? Because I was suddenly overcome with sadness.

The rest of that whole memory is pretty much an awful blur. The woman took me into an office that had nothing but a metal desk and a chair. There was a phone and some papers. If I close my eyes, I can see that green belt lying across that desk, curled like a snake. The fuzzy purple gloves right next to the belt. They were the only things with color in that whole room.

"Shoplifting is a very serious thing," the Kohl's lady told me. We were still waiting for my mother to come and get me. "It's a crime. If I report this to the police, it will go on your permanent record."

I think she wanted me to respond to this, or show more gratitude, but really I had no idea what my permanent record was.

"I'm really sorry," I said. I thought I was going to be sick.

"I know you are," she said. Her voice softened. "I can tell that you understand. You know, we catch teenagers in here all the time. Some kids act like they don't care."

I wasn't sure I knew what she was talking about, but the one thing I clearly understood was that this woman was being nice to me. I clung to that. I accepted her kindness, and I swore to myself I would never, never ever, ever again steal anything.

I never have.

My mother and the woman from Kohl's talked for a few minutes. God, they even hugged each other good-bye like they were old friends. Maybe the Kohl's lady had a totally messed-up teenage daughter too. Maybe they were comparing notes. How lucky. My mother loves to commiserate.

I guess, in retrospect, I could have been penitent, should have been humble and grateful and sorry. Maybe I would have been, too, if it weren't for the first thing my mother said to me when we got into the car. Before we even got out of the Kohl's parking lot.

"Why are you doing this to me?" she said. "Why?"

Part Two

I had been at Mountain Laurel three weeks. I thought my parents should ask for their money back since I was probably the only kid here who wasn't state funded. From what I could tell, Tommy's dad (who showed up Sunday evenings in a rusted-out Honda and threw his son and his cigarette butt out of the car with approximately the same amount of concern) wasn't paying the big bucks for Mountain Laurel's fine education that my parents were.

Carl got picked up and dropped off always in a different car, none of which looked like it was being driven by a grown-up. Carl said they were his cousins, and I swear when he got dropped off last time I saw something lying on the backseat.

"Was that a shotgun?" I asked him later.

"Yeah, so?" Carl said by way of an explanation.

I never got to see Billy's dad. I watched from my room, where I could see the barn and the garage and the driveway below. Sam would go to pick up Billy at the bus station in town. Billy brought his clothes from home in a big green trash bag. Sam was carrying it from the car and talking with Billy. There was just something in the way he held it that made you think Sam wouldn't have noticed if your stuff was in Gucci leather or Glad plastic. I could understand why everyone liked Sam.

When John came back it was a big production. I would have guessed they were John's mom and dad, even if John hadn't gotten out of the same car. First his mom popped out from one side and then his dad. Both of them were tall and big-boned. His mom wasn't ugly, but if I said she was the female version of John, it was true. And if you had never seen John before, you'd just think she was one of those women they called *handsome* in the old movies. (My grandmother still says that. She calls a woman *handsome*.)

John's mother had dark hair and a thick scarf around her neck. She was wearing a pleated skirt and thick tights and boots. John's dad was wearing a long black coat. And from the minute John stepped out from the backseat, both his parents had their arms around him. They snuggled up close. As stiff as John marched and as straight as his face remained, his parents laughed and kissed him and walked him all the way up to the

House. Each of them had a little suitcase in one hand and John's arm in the other.

Drew was always the last one to come back to Mountain Laurel. I watched out the window as a white Volvo station wagon with a DEFEAT BUSH sticker on the back bumper pulled into the driveway. A man got out. He was all white—white jacket, white shirt, white pants. Stark white hair standing up on all ends. He got out of the car and walked over to the passenger side. I could see Drew inside, crying. The man opened the door and gently urged Drew out. When Drew was standing but not moving, the man bent onto one knee and said something. Even from upstairs, behind the window, I could see Drew slowly begin to smile. Then the man wrapped his arms around Drew and hugged him, until Drew disappeared within the man's white clothing.

As soon as he let go, Drew went running up toward the House.

Mountain Laurel.
Where else? Nowhere. Nowhere. I was
just watching everyone coming back,
even though they didn't know I was
watching them. Marcella once told me
that her mother said God can see you

anywhere you are—which is why you should never do anything bad, Marcella said, even when you think you can get away with it. You shouldn't cheat or lie or pick your nose. Because God can see you.

So I said, Even when you're in the bathroom?

Marcella died laughing.

In second grade, I was Mrs. Eleanor Roosevelt.

It was a most coveted part. I mean, for some kid who liked stuff like that. Mrs. Rifkin didn't make a big deal about it. Thinking about it, Mrs. Rifkin didn't make a big deal about anything. She wasn't the kind of teacher who gushed all over you when you made a picture of a leopard and spent forty-five minutes drawing every single black spot. She didn't get all excited if your book report was five pages long instead of one. In a funny way, Mrs. Rifkin kind of reminded me of Gretchen, or the other way around.

I'm not sure if Mrs. Rifkin is even still alive. She was pretty old even back then. I know she's not teaching anymore. She retired after that year. We were her last second-grade class.

But Mrs. Roosevelt *was* the biggest part in the play. Bigger than being Mr. President Roosevelt, even. I had no idea Mrs. Rifkin was going to pick me. There was no talk about it. It wasn't a real play. It was just a scene from our reading books that Mrs. Rifkin thought would be fun to act out. No programs were going to be printed or refreshments planned, and no parents with video cameras were invited to take off from work and watch.

It was just for us.

And I was Mrs. Roosevelt. I think one important reason I got the part was because I was big. In second grade, I was one of the tallest girls. By fifth grade I was medium tall, and now I'm barely medium. I could also read easily, and in second grade that was still a fairly major and not entirely common achievement.

So for the sake of time constraints and smooth-going, I got the biggest part.

We did the play in the library, I remember. Mrs. Rifkin and Mrs. Dodge, the librarian, moved some chairs around and cleared out an area. We didn't have much room. The library aides were still walking around putting books back on the shelves. We stood with our books in our hands and read our lines.

"This will be a very difficult time," President Roosevelt (aka Josh Brogdan) said. Josh was wearing a tie over his T-shirt. Actually it was clipped to the collar of his T-shirt, weighing it down to expose the top of his skinny chest.

I was wearing a hat, I remember, a big hat with a feather that Mrs. Rifkin had brought from home. She said it was real. It had belonged to her great aunt Selma, but under that hat I became Mrs. Eleanor Roosevelt.

I looked down at my reading book and answered my husband, the president of the United States, circa 1941. "I know," I said.

There were about four parts in the scene and it lasted about twenty-five minutes. It would have been shorter except that right in the middle of the play, Hunter Cole had to go to the bathroom. When he got back we resumed. I don't remember very much. I can sort of see myself standing by one of the chairs that had been pushed aside. I remember feeling the weight of that big hat so that when I tipped my head the hat shifted but never fell off. I remember Josh because he was shorter than me. I remember it was fun. I remember feeling kind of important. No, I felt competent. Part of something that had gone well.

When we were done all the other kids clapped for a few polite seconds and then they made a fast break for the library doors (we had lunch the next period) until Mrs. Rifkin called everyone back to help set the room back up "the way we found it." One of the library aides was sitting in one of the seats. She had watched the whole play, apparently. She was standing in the back of the room where all the grown-ups usually stand.

"That was wonderful," she said, still clapping, looking straight ahead. "Wasn't it too bad the parents couldn't be here. It would have been really great if the parents had seen this. Don't you think?"

That's when the library aide lady turned to see who she had been talking to this whole time. She looked really surprised when she saw it was only me, like she had just given up some adult secret—that nothing counts unless a grown-up sees it or hears it, approves or disapproves.

Was that true? I remember thinking.

Or was it just a load of crap?

I didn't realize I was so used to seeing Drew at his window at night until he wasn't there. I was sitting up, looking out at the cold lawn and the empty chairs, and the black pond and the army of pine trees. Waiting. The sight of him, of his shadow by the window, had somehow become comforting to me. Weird, I know, but it's so easy to get used to something, anything maybe.

Except not wearing shoes.

But his light didn't come on.

I lay down in my bed and I sat up again. I pressed my hand to the cold glass but he still wasn't there.

When I asked him about it the next morning, he looked at me like he didn't know what I was talking about. Like he didn't know who I was.

"You know," I said. It was journal-writing time. Again. At Mountain Laurel it's either journal-writing, obeying-Gretchen, or eating time.

"You know, when you put your hand up on the window. Like you did when I first got here," I tried. "You know."

Drew was writing. He didn't say anything. I never saw what he wrote but he wrote pages of it. His hand-writing was really tiny and very neat. He had no para-graphs, no punctuation, or spaces of any kind. Just word after word after word.

He looked up at me.

"I don't know what you're talking about."

"Drew, c'mon. You're scaring me." I laughed.

There was something strange about his face. As if it had changed. As if he was challenging me: *Don't think you know who I am.*

I didn't say anything more. The next night he was

there again, at the window. I wasn't going to look. I wasn't going to wave back, but I did.

So some nights he was there and some he wasn't.

Monday we had a special art class at Mountain Laurel with a special guest teacher. I think she was an artist or something. I hope so for her sake, because she was a really lousy teacher. She called herself Ms. Dee and I got the feeling that was short for something she thought none of us would be able to pronounce.

First she gave a short lecture about self-portraits and meaning and the importance of true self-exploration. Then we saw some famous pictures in a book she held up. Van Gogh, with and without ear, Dürer and Rembrandt, looking very serious. All self-portraits. Then she handed out little mirrors for everyone.

For our self-portraits.

We had this class out in the barn where Sam usually worked, but today his stuff had been cleared away. One long table set on two sawhorses was pushed against the wall. All kinds of blades and electric power tools hung on the wall. Cords and hammers and drills.

Angel must have had his own corner in Sam's work-shop, and he wasn't about to give it up today. He had a small table and chair. He had a coffee cup and a book.

And he was sitting there, watching everyone invade his space.

"Finding the right medium is what this exercise is all about," Ms. Dee was saying. "I want everyone to walk around the room, which I've set up with different paints, markers, watercolors, and clay."

On the word *clay* Tommy and Carl, who up to this point had been flicking wood chips at each other, perked up.

Ms. Dee was apparently unaware that giving teenage boys unrestricted use of modeling clay was not an entirely terrific idea. So what happened was almost inevitable. I think there are just certain boys who revert to their caveman instincts when supplied with certain earth substances, like dirt and water.

In any case, when Tommy and Carl got a lump of moldable clay in their hands and a little loosely supervised time, it seemed they were capable of rendering only one phallic idol.

And then falling apart with laughter.

I didn't even have to *see* what they were making out of their clay.

I thought their idea of a self-portrait was perfectly fitting.

I wondered what the art teacher was going to do

when she caught them. For the time being she was trying to get Drew to choose a medium for his self-portrait. Actually she was first attempting to get him to come out from under the table where Billy and I were sitting. We had chosen some good old pencils and crayons.

"Pastels?" she suggested to Drew. Ms. Dee was young, but she had totally white hair. And she was very tall. She wore a long dress. I thought she looked pretty and different. She had a big beaded necklace on. But I shook my head. She was trying too hard, and it wasn't going to go over very well here. Maybe at my old school. Maybe she would have looked interesting. Or artsy.

But here she looked weak. The perfect target.

I could imagine back home, which kids would have tried to talk to her and ask her who her favorite artist was, what was her favorite museum in which European counties. Maybe I would have been one of them.

Ms. Dee's big earrings moved back and forth every time she moved her head, even the slightest bit.

"You can just draw. I have charcoals. Colored pencils? Or just use a regular pencil. Don't you want to draw? Do you want this mirror?" she said, bending down under the table. When Ms. Dee stood up again, I noticed her earring had gotten caught sideways in her hair and stayed like that.

Drew wouldn't come out.

"Well, when you're ready then," she said, as if hiding under a table was all part of the creative process, and she wandered away.

"Oh my God." I heard Ms. Dee from across the room and I knew she had made her way over to the clay table and seen what Carl and Tommy were creating. I must have been at Mountain Laurel too long. Unfazed, I continued to work on my picture.

"You're good," Billy said to me.

"No, I'm not. I can't draw faces."

"Well, it doesn't look that much like you, but it's good," Billy said, looking closely at my paper.

"Billy, it's not me. I can't draw people. I'm not going to. I'm just doodling."

"Oh, that explains why you look like a bird," Billy said.

I almost laughed, but he wasn't joking.

"Thanks," I said. I wanted to say something nice about Billy's but it was hard.

"Well, they will hate mine," Billy said.

"No, they won't," I said. "It's not bad."

Billy looked at me.

"I have that floating head thing. They hate the floating head thing," he said. "See my head-floating thing? They hate that."

Billy's drawing looked more like a five-year-old had done it than a twelve-year-old. It was messy and very plain. Two dots for eyes. An L for a nose. And sure enough, his head wasn't connected to the neck and shoulders he had drawn.

"They say it means something really bad when your head floats like that," Billy said. "But it's worse when you don't have a head at all."

"Why would you draw yourself without a head?"

Carl and Tommy were still trying very hard to justify their "self-portraits" to the teacher.

"No, no," Billy explained. "You have a face, but no head. Like eyes and a mouth but no circle around it. They think that's *really* crazy."

"Who's 'they'?" I had to ask.

Billy was trying to be very patient with me. He had taken to wearing short-sleeved army surplus shirts to better reveal his scar, which was now flat and dully red.

"You know, *them*," he said. "The ones who write all that stuff about you that gets put in your permanent record."

"Your what?" I asked.

"Your permanent record that gets put in Gretchen's file cabinet. You know?" Billy told me flatly.

"Her what?"

I didn't notice right away, but Drew had come out from under the table to stand next to us, listening and watching. He tried to help with the explanation. "The filing cabinet. In the office. Next to the kitchen."

Drew sat down and picked up a pencil.

"They hide money in there too. But that room is always locked," Billy said. "And candy."

I didn't really want to know how he knew that.

"I broke in there once," Billy said anyway.

"Well then, why don't you just connect the neck. Here." I pointed to the space on Billy's picture between his floating head and the two lumps that I thought were supposed to be shoulders. "Like just two longer lines or add a little shirt collar or something."

Billy just grinned.

Ms. Dee said art was the "act" of creating, not

the "result" of creating.

"We are too product oriented," she said. Her hoop earring had broken free as if to accentuate her words; it bounced against her cheek when she talked.

"You should enjoy the process and not worry if other people think your work is good or not," Ms. Dee went on. She wandered around the room encouraging us.

However, Ms. Dee *did* tell Carl and Tommy to put their "art" back into the clay bin even though they protested.

"I thought you said it didn't matter what other people thought," Carl tried. He wanted to keep his.

"But I was really enjoying the process," Tommy told her.

"Yeah, we all know you enjoy the process, about three times a day," Carl added, which was when Ms. Dee decided to forcefully take their creations away from them.

I watched as she made sure all the clay was totally smushed down before she closed the top of the bin. She took a moment to sort of compose herself. She ran her hands down the front of her smock and then, with a smile, began to circle around the room. I heard her kind of suck in her breath when she came around to Drew.

"Is this you?" she asked.

Drew shrugged.

"Wow," Billy said, leaning over. "You're *really* good."

"God, he's good," Carl said.

There was a little crowd around our table.

"It looks like a girl. Look at the hair," Tommy said over the tops of our heads. "I thought this was supposed to be a self-portrait."

"Drew is a girl," Carl added.

Even back at my school, being called a girl is apparently the utmost of insults.

"It isn't him," Ms. Dee said. She was studying the picture. Drew wasn't listening anymore. All of a sudden he was all alone. He had that look on his face. He was drawing quickly but very deliberately, very carefully.

I knew Ms. Dee wanted to tell him how good it was. How talented he was. But that would go against everything she had just lectured us about. She just watched.

I had to sit up in my seat and kind of lift myself up a little to see Drew's picture. It was beautiful. It was sad and simple, and every line moved together to create a face. At first you couldn't see it, but then you could. You had to look at it the right way; you had to not be looking for it. And then there it was.

"Jeez, she's right. It's not Drew," Billy said suddenly.

Everyone turned and looked.

It was my face. It was me.

Drew had offered it to me before I realized how much I wanted it. Like the perfume at the mall. Only this time it was a gift.

"You want it?" Drew asked me.

That's when everyone assumed it *was* a picture of me. As if that was proof.

"See," Billy said proudly. "I told you. It's Mia. It's a picture of Mia."

"It looks like she's a ghost," Carl said, standing toward the back of the crowd.

"She looks like a freakazoid."

"Shut up, faggot."

I don't know who was talking. Or to whom. But suddenly I was embarrassed by all the attention.

"No thanks, Drew. You keep it. It's fantastic. It's so great. You are really talented. You keep it. So you can remember me."

Drew sort of smiled and said, "Well, if you ever change your mind, it's yours."

He folded up the paper and put it in his back pocket.

But he never said it was a picture of me. He never actually said that.

Karen asked me this morning if I would help out in the nursery school because one of the aides was sick and couldn't come in.

"For the whole day?" I asked. That came out before I realized how it sounded.

But, in fact, I had had the chance to see the nursery-school kids in action. They usually got to Mountain Laurel around 9:00 a.m. We were already in the School House building, gardening or reading. But I knew the kids came in those special school buses. A lot of the kids came down out of the bus in a mechanical lift. There was always an aide to meet them. A couple needed wheelchairs.

I had seen two little girls, twins, I supposed, who clung to each other and walked into the nursery school like they were attached. They had oddly large heads and skinny little bodies.

All the nursery-school kids left around 3:00, before I went back up to my room. By then the nursery school was clean and quiet again.

"No," Karen answered. "I have a sub coming, but she can't get here until ten-thirty, eleven."

"I guess so," I said. "Sure."

Mary Belle was the head nursery-school teacher. I had seen her before too. She was usually there and setting up the nursery school, just after I had showered and was coming down from my room. She was one of those really, really friendly teachers who always smiles. She wore big, colorful dresses. She was kind of large. She had short, tight curly hair that always looked wet and shiny. She was pretty and always happy, it seemed.

She'd always be humming to herself as she put out puzzles and Play-Doh.

"Today we'll do water table," Mary Belle told me. "Thank you so much for helping. Can you get out those water toys and put them in there."

She pointed.

So far so good. No one had shown up yet. I helped get the room ready. I was familiar with some of the books and the little toys around the room. I used to love *Brown Bear Brown Bear, What Do You See?*

I had a really clear memory of coloring in little animals to go with that story in kindergarten and then reading the book with the teacher. This might not be so bad.

Then the kids came.

There was one aide for every two or three kids. So by the time everyone got off the bus and came into the room, there were about thirteen kids and five teachers. Including me.

Just getting everyone out of their coats and hats took a really long time. The kids with a lot of physical problems and the two in the wheelchairs had someone help them. Mary Belle told me to just wander around and help whoever needed it.

I turned to the cubbies. For a second I didn't move at all. I just stood there frozen. *Everyone* needed help. Except the two little twins. They were helping each other. That's right where I went first.

"Do you need any help?" I asked one of them.

"No," she answered. She was pulling her sister's arm out of her coat. The sleeve had turned inside out and gotten too tight. But that didn't stop her.

"Maybe if you slip it back on and take it off from the bottom," I tried. "Like this." I began to take the coat and pull it back up, but the girl immediately pulled away.

"I've got it," her sister said. "We don't need any help."

"We don't need any help," the sister with the stuck arm said.

I stepped back. There was a little boy behind me who was just standing there. He hadn't even taken his hat and gloves off. He was wearing snow pants and a jacket.

"Can I help you?" I said.

He didn't answer. He didn't even look at me.

I wondered if I should just start. Or would he get mad? Maybe I should ask him first.

"Hello," I said. I was sitting on the floor until I felt the cold and wetness from everyone's boots seeping into my pants. I quickly switched to kneeling.

"My name is Mia. Can I take off your coat for you?"

He still didn't answer.

I heard a big impatient huff from behind me. It was one of the sisters. The one who had snapped at me a second ago. She was definitely the leader of her twin set. Her sister stood nearby, but behind, just a tiny bit. They both had their coats, hats, and boots off and hung up.

I could see how really skinny they were. And there was an odd look to their faces, sort of like extra skin around their eyes. And they had big eyes.

"You're not doing it right," the leader said.

"Doing what right?"

She had her hands on her hips. "Damian won't talk to you unless you touch him," she told me.

"Touch him?"

She let out a big breath of air. She was totally exasperated. "You have to grab his face. But gently. Like this." She demonstrated on her sister, who burst out giggling, but I got the idea.

"Oh," I said. "Well, thank you. So what's your name?"

"My name is Ruth and my sister is Naomi," she told me. "It's from a Bible story. Now do you think you can handle this?"

I nodded and Ruth took her sister's hand.

"Oh, by the way, I'm Mia," I said before they turned and headed for the water table.

Ruth stopped and looked at me.

"We know that," she said. "You live upstairs."

Cecily had this freak thing wrong with her when she was a baby, not even a year old. One day she kept lifting up her left leg, like she didn't want to put weight on it or like it hurt. So my mom took her to the doctor, who didn't know what it was, so he sent us to another doctor and then another and another all the way up to an oncologist, which, I found out at six years old, is a cancer doctor.

If Cecily had been able to talk, it certainly would have helped. But while her twenty-plus-word vocabulary did (naturally) place her in a very high percentile for intelligence (actually measured), it didn't allow her to tell us what was wrong with her leg.

Nothing.

It turned out to be nothing. After a bunch of X rays, bone scans and blood tests, they found that nothing was wrong with her leg. It must have been some tiny fracture that elevated some tiny blood protein. Whatever.

It was nothing.

She was fine. But for a while, for about a month or so, things were awful. Just the thought of what might have been, what could have been. It stayed with our family for a long time.

That's what my morning in the nursery school was. It was the might have been and the could have been. Not that any of these kids had cancer, but almost all of them had medical problems. They had brain defects and physical handicaps, learning disabilities and alcoholic mothers who drank themselves into oblivion all through their pregnancies.

That's what the twins had, fetal alcohol syndrome. Mary Belle told me.

"Do you ever worry that there are only so many words in the world?" Drew asked me. We were walking from the School House to the House for lunch. It was only a couple of days until Thanksgiving break, a couple of days and I would have been at Mountain Laurel for one month. I would get to go home this weekend.

It was so cold, my cheeks were pinched. My scalp was cold. Everyone else was way ahead. They were probably inside already. Warm. Warm*er*. I stayed back with Drew.

"What do ya mean?" I asked. I was trying to hurry, but Drew was slow.

"Well, just technically speaking, there are only a finite number of words in any language, right?" Drew asked me.

"Yeah, I guess so."

"So then one day," Drew said, "everything that can ever be said will be said. And every book that could ever be written will be."

"Hmmm."

I suppose I wasn't really listening. I was too cold, and besides, half the things Drew (or anybody here) said were crazy. And sometimes with Drew, if you didn't agree with him, he took it the wrong way. Like you didn't like him, or like he had said something wrong, and he'd get upset. Or he'd just slip away and forget he had been talking to you at all. So sometimes it was better to just listen and pretend to agree.

"And it's the same with music, isn't it?" Drew talked as we walked.

"With music?"

"Yeah," Drew went on. "If there are only a certain number of musical notes, then, someday, no matter how far in the future that is, someday, every possible combination of musical notes will have been put together. And there will be no new songs."

"But there are so many combinations." I wanted to reassure him.

"But there is no such thing as infinite," Drew was saying. "There has to be a finish to everything. An end."

I blew my warm breath into my hands. "Maybe, but it's more than your brain could ever even imagine. That will never happen in your lifetime."

"Maybe not mine," Drew said.

I wasn't sure if Drew was referring to his lifetime or his brain.

I was just about to ask him, but when we got up onto the porch we could hear John screaming. Yelling angrily, urgently. His voice was so strange, high-pitched and frightening. It hardly sounded like him at all. Drew and I looked at each other, both wondering, I suppose, what John would be capable of doing if he ever lost control.

We hurried into the mudroom. I took off my shoes without even thinking about it. I had started keeping an extra pair of socks in my coat pocket, and I slipped them on.

We could hear Karen's voice now. And Gretchen's. Gretchen was telling Carl to go and find Sam. A second later, Carl brushed by us. He didn't even grab his coat from the mudroom.

"John's gone crazy," Carl said. He flew out the door. *Gone* crazy?

* * *

John had been caught cheating on his life.

* * *

Apparently, Karen had had her suspicions, turned over those folded-over pages marked PRIVATE in John's writing journal, and read them.

She discovered that John had been asking Maggie about her plans for the week's menu not just because he was weird (which he was) but because he had been writing his daily journal entries a week in advance. The only missing piece of information (in John's mind) that could have possibly altered the events of any given day would be what he would be eating for breakfast, lunch, and dinner. Breakfast was a no-brainer since John never had anything but the oatmeal, which was always a Mountain Laurel option. Lunch and dinner, however, posed a serious problem. Cornering Maggie and getting the week's menu seemed to be the perfect solution. Once he had this information, John could pretty much construct his entire week and get all his homework done by Monday afternoon.

That's exactly what John had been doing. Rather successfully. But when Karen told him he couldn't do this anymore, he went, as Carl had aptly put it, crazy.

"You weren't supposed to look," John was yelling. He was stamping his feet. His big feet.

"That's not the point, John," Karen was saying.

We were all standing in the den. Everyone had heard the yelling and wandered in. It was almost as if the level of noise made the space smaller and John look bigger.

"What is the point, if that is not the point? That is the point," John said. "When I turned down the page . . . You said that. You promised. You said that. That is the point."

Gretchen held on to John's arm. I thought if he had

wanted, he could have lifted his arm and taken Gretchen right along with it. He could have flung her right across the room. He was pulling away, but somehow she held on and stayed on the floor.

"John, you are right. That *is* what Karen said. And Karen was wrong for what she did. But that doesn't make what you did right. Does it?" Gretchen said.

"Why not?" John said. "I didn't do anything wrong." He finally freed his arm and began pacing around the room. Everyone backed away and gave him space.

"John," Gretchen said firmly. "Sit down. Right now. In this chair." She pointed. She ordered.

John stopped pacing for a moment. He looked as if he was considering the chair, but then he started shouting again.

"It's not right. That's not what she said. That's not what she said. I didn't do anything wrong. She did." John pointed to Karen.

Karen stepped forward a bit. "I'm sorry, John. You're right. I shouldn't have looked ahead. But I just want you to understand . . ."

"No, *you* need to understand!" John said. His anger had a target. It probably should have been Carl or Tommy or even Billy for all the teasing and torture, but at that moment it was Karen.

"Why is it wrong to be prepared? What is wrong with that!" John shouted.

"What the hell is he talking about?" Tommy whispered to no one in particular.

Trying to do exactly the same thing every day, exactly the same way, was apparently John's one and only goal. Something about that concept terrified me.

Not just that someone would want to know what they were going to do every day, know exactly what to expect and be prepared for it. But the more disturbing aspect was that somehow putting it in writing, committing it to paper, writing it in a journal would make it happen. Would permanently seal your fate, so to speak. Make it unalterable. Make it real.

"John, if you sit down, I will talk to you about it," Gretchen said. "I will listen."

Maybe John would have sat down at that point. And it might have all been over. John lowered his arms and took a deep breath, but that was precisely when Carl returned, with Sam right behind him.

"See!" Carl shouted. "There he is."

John felt the urgency and accusation leveled right at him. There was really nothing else for him to do but run.

* * *

Everyone had a direction to search. Sam and Angel went in the truck out the back road. Half an hour had passed and John had not returned. Carl, Drew, and Mr. Simone looked in the School House building. There were rooms in there that no one used where John might be hiding. Billy and Maggie had the House and the dorms. Karen and Tommy took the nursery-school building, upstairs and down. Gretchen sat in her chair and waited for reports.

I had the barn.

"John?" I called out as I walked inside.

On the far end, the wall that faced the pond was so worn and old that rotten boards were half missing. You could see right outside. You could see the cliff that led down to the pond. In fact, it looked like the whole barn was teetering on the edge of a cliff. There wasn't anything particularly safe about this barn. I didn't think anyone trying to escape would come here. I turned to leave when I heard a thump.

"John?" I said again.

"What?" John answered. He was still mad.

"Everybody is looking for you," I said. I couldn't see him, but it sounded like he was up in the loft.

"I know."

"So come down," I said. I stepped into the center of

the barn and looked up. I still couldn't see him.

"No."

For a moment I didn't know what to do. If I went to get help, John might run away again. Maybe farther. Maybe toward the pond or the pine forest. I knew there were hundreds of acres of land back there. John didn't seem like the type who would survive out in the woods for more than a minute or two.

Neither was I, for that matter.

If I called out for help, John might freak out again. And nobody would hear me from here anyway. If I stood long enough, I could probably signal to Mr. Simone when I saw him coming out. He'd have to walk by this way.

"Who's there?" John's voice came out of the corner shadow in the loft.

"Me."

"Who's 'me'?"

I looked out to the School House building, but I didn't see anyone around to help. There was just me.

"Mia," I answered.

"Mia?"

"Yeah."

I could hear John starting to move. His weight made the barn creak loudly.

"Come down. Everybody is worried," I tried again.

"No. Karen was wrong and I was right. She never said you couldn't write ahead in your journal. She never said you couldn't do that."

That was true.

"You're right," I said.

"She said she would never read something if you turned the page down. She lied," John said. He really was angry. "If someone says something, they should mean it."

"You're right," I said. "That sucks."

I could see his foot, his huge foot sticking out. He was edging toward the ladder like he had more to say and wanted me to listen.

"What's wrong with what I did?" John asked me. "What's wrong? I didn't hurt anybody."

"No, of course not," I said. "You know teachers. They just get like that."

I thought I could just take his side, whatever he said. Then he'd trust me and come down. It was cold in the barn. I wanted to go already.

"Like what?" John said. "What do you mean? They get like *what*?"

I realized I had said the wrong thing. I was making it worse.

"Well, I mean. . ." But I didn't know what I meant. I

had to choose my words more carefully. I had to think about what I was saying.

"Karen was wrong and I was right," John said. I heard him moving around up there. He wasn't exactly light-footed.

"Well, wait a minute, John. Think about it."

"What?"

"Well, if you write everything down before it really happens, then you can't change anything," I said. "You don't have any choices."

"I don't want any choices. I know what I want to do. Every day. I just want people to let me alone so I can do it."

I could hear tears behind his rough voice.

"I know. I know. I mean, so do I. Everybody does. Everybody wants to be left alone, but what if? What if there was something that you didn't know you wanted to do yet? What if there was something to do that might be really good? Good for you, something you'd really like but you wouldn't even try because it wasn't written in your journal?"

"Like what?"

Now, this was hard. I shrugged to buy time, even though John couldn't see me. *Like what?*

"Like maybe a new edition of *The Guinness Book of*

World Records comes out and—"

John interrupted me. "The next edition won't be published until next September eighth."

Oh.

"But there might be something, John. Something. Just because you wrote it down doesn't mean you won't change your mind. I mean . . . I mean, wouldn't it be worse if you had to go back and erase?"

I stopped. I couldn't think of anything more to say because there were certainly some things you could never go back and erase. But I didn't think John would be able to handle that.

I used to think I couldn't either.

Sometimes lately, I think maybe I can.

"Yeah, that really would be worse," John said as we were walking together back to the House. He was completely calm, as if nothing had happened at all. His voice sounded normal again, although I use the word *normal* very loosely. It's all relative, I guess.

"I hate erasing," John told me.

"Me too," I said.

In a way it was funny, with everything that happened with John and how upset everyone had gotten and how well it had all turned out, that it was Drew who fell out the window that night.

Of course, there was nothing funny about it.

Sam had found Drew, half naked and totally unconscious, lying in the bushes outside the House. His pajama bottoms were left behind (so to speak), hooked onto one of the young birch trees that Gretchen recently had planted around her house to block some of the cold winds that blew down from the pine-covered mountain. The birch tree bent, caught Drew, and ever so gently dropped him nearly to the ground, but not quite. Not until the pajama bottoms tore and Drew fell the rest of the way and passed out. But he was fine.

Only then was it funny.

Hilarious.

At least the boys at Mountain Laurel thought so.

Mountain Laurel, it seems, has had more than its share of accidents, and they were all hilarious. Two years ago, according to Tommy, there was a kid here who shot a neighbor with a BB gun.

"Right in the ass," Tommy told me when he could stop laughing long enough to speak.

"What happened to him?" I asked. We were in the dining room, all early for some reason. Technically, right before lunch was our free time, but no one seemed to want to be alone. Hearing Maggie working in the kitchen was comforting. Drew's seat was empty.

"What happened to who? The kid or the guy walking down the road?"

"Both."

Tommy was enjoying the spotlight, the holder of memory. "Well, the guy walking his dog down the road, the guy who got nailed in the ass"—Tommy paused for the giggles—"he was fine. He didn't even press charges. But the kid who did it got kicked out."

"That very day," Carl added.

I guessed that Tommy and Carl had been going to Mountain Laurel for a while.

"Well, that doesn't really sound like an accident," I said. I could practically see the whole scene: gun, ass, running, Gretchen. It was easy to imagine.

"It was," Tommy insisted. "He wasn't *aiming* at that guy. It was an accident."

"How did he get that BB gun here?" Billy wanted to know. "How did he get it past Gretchen?"

"Shut up, faggot" was Carl's answer.

Maggie banged a pot in the kitchen. It was an "appropriate language" warning. Who knew she was listening?

"And remember last year? That kid Red?" Tommy was saying.

"*Reed*, you jerk-off," Carl gently corrected him.

"Yeah, Reed. Remember him?"

Most of the boys at the table did. Even John was nodding his head. I noticed only Angel wasn't participating in the Mountain Laurel revelry.

"Remember when Reed cut his head open?" Tommy went on.

"Yeah, there was blood everywhere," Billy jumped in. "That's because the head bleeds a lot, you know. But that was a fight, and a fight's not an accident either. But my arm was an accident, remember? Mine was . . ."

Billy looked like he was all geared to go on, to describe Reed's wound or maybe his own, but suddenly Angel said something. I think it was the first time I'd heard him talk since my first night when Gretchen made everyone say hello.

"Drew's wasn't an accident," Angel said. He had a lyrical Puerto Rican accent. He spoke slowly and softly. "He was trying to kill himself."

"That's not true," I said. I stood up.

And for some reason John, who now saw himself as my defender, stood up as well. He towered over Angel.

"He was not," John said, although I doubt he understood.

But Angel didn't flinch. "You think Drew just got up at four-thirty in the morning, walked over to the window in the hall when it's thirty-five degrees out, opened it up, and oops. Fell?"

"Maybe he was trying to run away," Carl said.

"Then why wouldn't you just walk down the stairs and out the front door? There are no alarms here. Everybody knows that. And what . . . who is going to chase you . . . Gretchen?"

It figured that Angel would have all the details. The time. The exact window. He'd probably heard it while hanging out with Sam. Besides, people who talk the least hear the most.

"Well, she does have that big dog," Billy said. He started laughing . . .

Until Tommy, who was sitting next to Billy, whacked him on the shoulder, not too hard. Just enough to make Billy's eyes tear up. Billy didn't say anything. He didn't even rub his arm up and down like he would usually do.

"You don't know it, though. Not for sure. You don't know anything," I said to Angel.

"He left a note," Angel said.

No one said anything after that.

I wasn't surprised at all when Billy came to me with his head down and his hand out. He was certainly always one for the dramatic. He handed me Drew's picture.

"He said you could have it, remember?" Billy told me. "I thought you'd want it now."

"Billy. He's not dead."

"Yeah, but still. I found it in his room." Billy held it out to me. "He wanted you to have it, remember? Take it."

And I took it.

It's hard to say exactly what I now found disturbing about Drew's picture. Something about the face; it seemed to change every time you looked at it. Suddenly it looked more like Drew.

It wasn't one of those really realistic drawings where you can see every facial line and every hair follicle. But it wasn't abstract, either, with a square head and two eyes on one side of the face. It was something else entirely, almost like it was more about the sad expression on the face than the face itself. It was more

about what was inside the person's mind than outside.
So in a way it could have been anyone.

Mountain Laurel.

Where else?

Gretchen let everyone stay up
later than usual. Even though they
kept telling us Drew was going to be
all right. He was in the hospital. He
didn't even have one broken bone.
They never said he did it on purpose,
but they never said he didn't.

I know Drew didn't want to die.
It's not that high a window. He didn't
want to die, but he wanted something. He just didn't know what it
was. Maybe he went looking for it. I
can understand that.

That is certainly a reasonable
thing to do. In a way.

The office was easy to break into. I figured if Billy
could do it, I could certainly do it. It was just like in the
movies where the guy takes an unbent paper clip and
wriggles it around in the lock for a couple of seconds. It

worked. The office door clicked open.

I walked into the dark room. The shades on all three windows were pulled down. I had been in here only once before. Almost four weeks ago, when I first got here and Karen was showing me around.

Four weeks? How could so much have happened in four weeks? And so little? Four weeks back home and I'd probably have taken seven or eight quizzes, at least two tests. A social studies project. Probably science, too. Four Current Events. Six or seven volleyball games—even more practices. A book report or two.

My head was spinning with two worlds that didn't make any sense. And now I found myself standing in Gretchen's office, in front of her file cabinet. If there was a place where two worlds met, it would be in those files.

The file cabinet wasn't even locked, as it turned out. The manila folders were just squished in, one behind the other, with a little tab sticking up. I pulled out the drawer.

They were in alphabetical order, by last name. Lots of names I hadn't heard of, maybe students long gone. It took me awhile to find a name I recognized.

John.

Katzenbaum, John.

Was that *John*? I didn't even know his last name. There were a bunch of folders with "John" as the first name. Then I noticed colored tabs pasted onto the folders. I rifled through. There was only one Angel. One Carl.

All those folders had blue stickers. Current students?

So this one must be John. And this one was Carl's. Carl Mlasek. I pulled it out.

Carl Mlasek
Age 14–Conduct Disorder

Diagnosis: Adolescent Antisocial Behavior

I shut Carl's folder and quickly slipped it back where I had taken it from. I pulled out another folder and another, always careful to note which name came before and after. Careful to replace it exactly where it had been. I looked them over pretty quickly, one by one, before someone could come in and find me.

Tommy Dwyer

Age 13

Diagnosis: Oppositional Defiant Disorder

Billy Sisco

Age 10

*Diagnosis: Attention-deficit/Hyperactivity Disorder
and Adjustment Disorder*

Angel Rosario

Age 15

*Diagnosis: Depressive Disorder not otherwise
specified*

John Katzenbaum

Age 15

*Diagnosis: Obsessive-compulsive Disorder/
Autism not otherwise specified*

I put John's folder back and stood looking at all the files. I checked over all the labels, with blue and yellow and red stickers. Some looked like they were so old and had been read so many times, the tippy part where the name goes was wobbly and wrinkled, about to break right off. Drew's was one of those. I pulled it out. I sat down on the floor right there and began reading.

Drew Keeping
Age 11
Diagnosis: Associative Personality Disorder

His folder was so thick. There were a lot of papers inside. Forms and what looked like samples of writing and even drawings. The top sheet had Mountain Laurel letterhead. It was several pages long, stapled together. It talked about Drew's personality profile. School records. Grades. Teacher comments. Scores on tests I had never heard of. And there was a long family history written in messy handwriting. I tried to follow it.

Mother — whereabouts unknown
Father — unknown

Apparently Drew was living with a foster dad, Bradley Cotes. (That must have been the man in white with the white Volvo.) Drew's mother had a history of mental illness. She had been homeless for several years when Drew was a baby and a toddler, moving from shelter to shelter, sometimes living on the street. There had been a variety of men in her life; incidents of abusive behavior toward both Drew and his mother were likely although not substantiated.

It went on and on.

I had to close the folder. There were so many reasons, I guess. Too many. You could see them all here. Drew had more than enough reasons to do what he did, if that's really what he did.

You could have written a depressing twenty-page paper on Drew's life. And yet, somehow, it still didn't explain—why? I knew he hadn't meant it. But if I concentrated and read and studied every note and letter and test score in this folder, would it make a difference? Would I understand?

He didn't want to die; he wanted answers.

And so, what about me?

Did I have a folder?

A permanent record?

I slipped Drew's folder back into place and looked for my name. So this is what the lady at Kohl's had meant. This was my permanent record. Hadn't she promised me I wouldn't have one? Wasn't that the deal? I watched my own fingers rapidly pulling the file tabs back, *P*s and *Q*s and *R*s and finally the *S*s.

So I do have a permanent record. Here it is.

SINGER, MIA.

It was thin. There were only two pieces of paper in it. One was from my old school, a single sheet of paper, a computer printout of all my grades from sixth grade. The other was a form. It had my mother's handwriting on it.

> *Mia Singer*
> *Age 13*
> *Mother — Leslie Singer*
> *Father — Bob Singer*

It had my birthday. My address. It listed emergency numbers. It had that stupid therapist's name and number. Siblings. It had Cecily's name and age.

And that was all.

"Is that your file?"

I looked up. "Yes," I said. I wasn't afraid. It suddenly seemed odd that I ever could have been.

"It's not nearly as interesting as you thought, is it?" Gretchen asked me.

"No. It's boring."

Gretchen stood at the doorway.

"That's good," she said. "Boring is good. Did you find

what you were looking for?"

"Yeah," I said. "I think I did."

I noticed Gretchen was using a cane. She was not the type to slouch or lean against a door frame. But you could tell it was difficult for her to stand.

I was still sitting on the floor with my folder in my hands. I looked down as Gretchen made her way into the tiny office and lowered herself into a chair by the desk.

"Mia, don't worry so much," she told me. "You'll find your way."

She rested her cane next to her. I had never been this close to her. Her skin looked loose, almost soft, so pale. Her eyes were blue. I don't think I noticed that before.

"I'm not sure," I said.

"I'm sure," Gretchen said. "I've seen plenty of young people in my day. I'm older than I look, you know."

Was Gretchen making a joke?

Sitting on the floor, I had to look up to see her face. She was smiling. Really smiling, almost laughing.

"How old are you?" I asked her.

She laughed. "Old enough," she said. "Old enough to be sure. And old enough to know most things you have to learn for yourself."

Then Gretchen put her bony hands on the sides of the chair and started to lift herself. I got up quickly and put my hand out to help her.

"But now remember, my dear. Don't try so hard. You'll see. In life you move toward the things you like and away from what you don't," Gretchen said.

"It's that easy?" I asked her. Her arm was so skinny and fragile, but I could feel her weight like determination.

"Yes, it's that easy," she said. Then she laughed. "The hard part is to just keep moving." She took her cane and, with just the slightest movement of her elbow, I knew she wanted me to let go.

And then very slowly, one step and one click of her cane at a time, Gretchen headed back to her chair in the living room. I waited until she was gone. Then I picked up my file from the floor, slipped it back into the cabinet, and shut the drawer tight.

Part Three

Mountain Laurel.

This is going to be my last journal
entry. I'm going home. But you can
keep this journal and my pictures if
you want.

I didn't have that much to say.
Did I?

It was more about listening.

My mother came to pick me up from Mountain
Laurel the day before Thanksgiving. It was snowing
pretty hard. My mother hates to drive in the snow. She
doesn't like to drive over bridges. Tunnels, forget it.

Maybe it's all part of her nervous, crazy, overprotective personality.

But she got here.

My mother didn't talk for nearly the whole first half
hour of our drive—unheard of for her. My mother has a
hard time with silences. I knew she was keeping quiet for

me. I knew she had a hundred questions. A million things she wanted me to say. She also knew I didn't want to talk. Not yet.

For the first time in forever, I was the first one to speak.

"Are we going to stop and get something to eat?"

She jumped right on it. Maybe a little too quickly, but it was okay.

"Are you hungry?" she asked me.

It was snowing a lot less here. The sun was even beginning to shine. She was a little more relaxed. She had stopped gripping the steering wheel with her two fists.

"Sure," I said.

"I think there's a place around here. I saw it when I was driving up."

It looked to me like we were in the middle of nowhere. For the last twenty minutes we had passed nothing but trees and highway exits that seemed to lead to more nowhere.

"There," my mother said. She pointed. It was a sign, just a little smaller than a highway billboard. It looked handmade, and it was nailed to a phone pole.

JUST ANOTHER ROADSIDE ATTRACTION, it said. That was the name of the place. You could see the little restaurant just off the highway, like a log cabin almost.

My mother said, "It's cute, isn't it?"

I agreed.

She pulled the car into the parking lot. There were only a couple of other cars. When we walked in, the two people at the counter looked up at us and then went back to their breakfast. We had our choice of booths. They were all empty. We both plopped down on either side of the table. The waitress came by, poured my mother some coffee, and asked if we needed a little more time.

"Yes, please."

We both looked at our menus for a while, and then I thought I heard a little giggle come from my mother's side of the table. She had the menu covering her face.

"What?"

"Remember when . . . ," my mother began. "No, it's silly. Forget it."

"No, what?" I reached over and pulled her menu down. "What?"

She was laughing again. "Well, I was just thinking. Remember when you were really little and you'd eat everything on your plate in a certain order and you'd have to eat everything of that one thing before you'd move on?"

I did that. "I remember," I said.

"Well," she said. "I just remember that I used to think

you were eating the thing you liked the most first."

But that wasn't true.

I always ate the thing I liked least first. I got it out of the way. I did what I had to do, and then I rewarded myself.

"So for the longest time, for years," my mother went on, "I thought you were this wonder child who loved vegetables. I remember you'd eat up all your broccoli really fast. Remember?"

"Yeah," I said.

"So I kept making broccoli. Every night, remember?" She started laughing again. "For years!" she blurted out.

"I hate broccoli," I said.

"I know!" This time she laughed so hard her coffee almost came spitting out of her mouth.

I handed her a napkin. "God, Mom. What's so funny?"

"I had it all wrong," she said. She suddenly looked more like she was going to cry. "I didn't know. Isn't it kind of funny? I had it all wrong."

She was laughing and crying at the same time.

Then she said quietly, "I didn't know."

I looked around to see if anyone was watching us, but there wasn't anybody else in the whole place. The two people at the counter must have left. I got up from my seat and sat down next to my mother in the booth so we were both facing the same way. It probably looked really weird.

"Thanks," my mother said. She wiped her eyes.

When the waitress came by, we ordered. My feet were just starting to warm up. My mom told me little things about Cecily and Dad. She told me Marcella calls every night and asks when I'm coming back. That made me feel good.

"Mom?" I said after a beat.

"Uh-huh?"

"I don't want to go back."

"You don't have to," she said. "I never wanted you to go."

"I thought you did," I said.

"I didn't know," my mother said. "I guess I'm still getting it wrong."

"Not always," I told her. "You've just got to let me make my own mistakes."

"It's hard," she said. But she nodded.

And then our food came, just in time, because I was just about done with this kind of talking. Just as we were finishing, people started showing up and sitting in the booths around us, and the waitress dropped our bill on the table. It was probably getting close to lunchtime.

"Ready?" my mom asked me.

"Definitely."

My mom started fishing around in her bag for her wallet. She took about a million things out and clunked them on the table. A two-hundred-year-old hard candy with no wrapper rolled off the table and landed on the floor.

God, nobody can embarrass me like my mother.

Finally she got everything settled. She got the money figured out and she got her makeup, used tissues, Chap-Stick, loose change, old receipts, and Cecily's retainer (What was that doing in there?) back into her bag. She was holding the check and her money, waiting for the waitress to come back around. So she could pay. And we could go home.

I didn't expect to feel the way I did when we drove up the hill and made the turn onto our street. As we came around the corner I saw the sign. It was a red and white real-estate sign swinging from two chains, attached to a sturdy white post. Right on the front lawn.

Debbie Sanders's house was for sale.

My mother saw the sign too, and she looked over at me.

"I know," she said.

It was so sad. I didn't know if Debbie's family was

· 162 ·

giving up or moving on. Or just moving. But it made me so sad to see their house for sale.

DREAMING AND NOT DREAMING

I imagine myself just walking right into Debbie's house. Somehow, I sneak inside and walk up the carpeted stairs. I just imagine the stairs are carpeted because I've never really been in Debbie's house.

Now I see the bathroom at the top of the landing. It is spotless, and there is even a little candle burning on the sink. Vanilla. I guess they want things to look nice; after all, the house is for sale.

The first bedroom on the left is obviously the master bedroom. The bed is made, not too many pillows. There is a little lamp with the light on, next to the bed. The books on top of the TV are neat. There are not too many knickknacks. I bet there was more stuff around before some real-estate agent told them to "unclutter." It makes the house look bigger. It will sell faster, she would have told them.

And that's all they wanted.

Then I walk to the next bedroom and it is a mess. I know at once this is Debbie's room.

It's been almost a year but everything is exactly the way Debbie left it the night she was supposed to go to the volleyball dinner. She was in too big a hurry.

Debbie's bed is unmade. Her faded jeans and sweatshirt are half on the bed and half on the floor. A spiral notebook is open on her bed, and there is even a pencil right next to it. A math problem halfway to being solved is left on the page.

Her stuffed animals are squeezed between her bed and the wall like she hadn't bothered to take them off the bed before she went to sleep the night before. Another pile of her volleyball practice jersey and sneakers sits in the corner by the door, on their way to the laundry basket, but they didn't make it.

Her life is all around me. Her life is my life. And my life is hers. And I can't tell the difference anymore. She has, I count them, fifteen trophies on her bureau. She has a picture of her and her two best friends, Jamie and Alison, at another friend's birthday party. They all have their arms around one another and they are smiling that huge, totally happy, totally genuine smile of friendship and all possibilities.

I sit down on Debbie's bed because it seems like the right thing to do.

"Mia?" Suddenly Mrs. Sanders is standing in the doorway. "Mia Singer?" But she doesn't seem surprised to see me.

I imagine she looks older than the last time I saw her at school or a game or something. She looks more tired. She sits down right next to me on the bed.

"You were on the volleyball team with Debbie, weren't you?" she asks me.

I nod my head.

"And your family lives just up the street, right?"

"Yeah, we do."

"What are you doing here?"

"I don't know," I tell her. "I'm sorry if I upset you. It's just, when I saw your house for sale . . . I don't know . . . It made me sad."

"Me too," Mrs. Sanders says.

"I always wanted to tell you how sorry I was. I never got to tell you. I'm so sorry. It must have been the most horrible thing in the whole world."

"It is."

I imagine this scene almost every time I drive by Debbie Sanders's house and I see the FOR SALE sign. I imagine this story or some version of it, of Debbie's room and Debbie's mother, but even as I do I know that one day, probably soon, a new family will buy this house and move in. And one day, long after that, I will stop thinking of Debbie quite so often.

But I won't completely stop. Never completely.

At Debbie's funeral we were pressed shoulder to shoulder, right up to the wall. There were so many of us kids in that outer room that it was really uncomfortable.

We all had to stand, and you started to feel guilty that your feet were hurting. Lots of different people spoke at Debbie's funeral, and it was all broadcast through these big, huge speakers hanging on either side of the lobby. Debbie's father was the last one to talk. There is something really awful about hearing a man cry. It shakes you to the core. I could hear the pain in his voice, and I could see it in everyone's eyes around me.

Debbie's father talked about Debbie, about when she was little, about her spirit and her personality. Just like everyone before him had. He had some personal stories and memories that he could barely choke out.

"If I could go back and do it all over again—," he said. "If I could go back and have every one of those wonderful days and every one of the difficult days, if I could have any of those minutes and seconds with Debbie again, even if I knew how it was going to end, even if I knew that she was going to die that day . . . I would do it all over again. In a heartbeat. I would do it all over again, every time."

In a heartbeat.
Every time.

Home.

I'm going to start a new journal.
But it's not for school. This one is
just for me. I won't have to fold over
any pages or cheat on my life. Just
write every now and then, if I feel
like it.

See if I have anything to say.

By the way, school has been okay.

I like to tell different stories
about where I was for a month at the
beginning of this year. I make up crazy
stories about what it was like there
and really freak people out. Sometimes
Marcella gets in on the joke.

"My mother had to have me kidnapped from this
cult and have me deprogrammed . Yeah, it could happen
to anyone. It's called Stockholm syndrome or something
like that."

That was a pretty good one.

"I was at this place where they dropped you off in
the woods, like a hundred miles from civilization. All we
had was our tents, and some food, a rope, and an axe.

It's, like, about survival. Oh yeah . . . there were bears. Tons of them."

That one was okay. But Marcella and I had our favorite.

"No, no. It's true. She really was at that famous rehab place, the one where all the movie stars go. Really. I saw the pictures," Marcella says. "She was in the room right next to that twin. You know which one. Yeah, the skinny one, the one with brown hair."

But when we are alone, Marcella asks me to tell

her everything.

We are lying on the matching beanbag chairs in Marcella's room. I can hear her brother's video game coming through from the room next door.

Marcella bangs on the wall. "Turn it down," she shouts.

It is all very familiar and comforting.

"So?" Marcella asks.

"Nothing. It's dumb stuff. Boring," I say.

"But I want to know," she says.

What can I tell her? What do I really know? Karen has written to me twice since I didn't go back to Mountain Laurel. John is no longer writing a week ahead in his journal, although he does focus primarily on what he will be having for breakfast, lunch, and dinner. He talks about me a lot, Karen wrote me. So do all the boys. Billy misses me, she wrote. And they've gotten two new boarding students at Mountain Laurel. Two girls. They are both terrified of Gretchen. I had to smile when I read that.

And Drew?

Drew is doing better. He is in a different school now where they can keep a closer watch on him, where he can get the help he needs. I'm not so sure about that. But Karen told me he's drawing a lot. Apparently Drew is extremely talented, a true prodigy. Someone from *60 Minutes* wants to do a show on him.

That makes me smile too.

"C'mon, tell me," Marcella is asking me.

But it's hard to explain. It's a little embarrassing. Mostly confusing. I have Drew's picture. It's folded up again, just the way he stuffed it into his pocket. I don't think I'll ever show anyone. But it's there. And sometimes I take it out and just look at it.

Try to figure out who it is.

So I say, "Does it really matter?"

"Yeah, it does," Marcella answers, and I know she is right.

It's all crazy.
And there will always be things I can't erase.
But I think the best I can do
is defy the craziness for as long as I can.
And live.
And be happy.
Peace.